DESERT JOURNEY

DESERT JOURNEY

LAURAN PAINE

WHEELER
CHIVERS

This Large Print edition is published by Wheeler Publishing, Waterville, Maine, USA and by BBC Audiobooks Ltd, Bath, England.
Wheeler Publishing, a part of Gale, Cengage Learning.

The text of this Large Print edition is unabridged.
Other aspects of the book may vary from the original edition.
Set in 16 pt. Plantin.
Printed on permanent paper.

LIBRARY OF CONGRESS CATALOGING-IN-PUBLICATION DATA
Paine, Lauran. 　　Desert journey / by Lauran Paine. 　　　　p. cm. — (Wheeler Publishing large print Western) 　　　　ISBN-13: 978-1-59722-745-2 (softcover : alk. paper) 　　　　ISBN-10: 1-59722-745-5 (softcover : alk. paper) 　　　　I. Title. 　　PS3566.A34D47 2008 　　813'.54—dc22　　　　　　　　　　　　　　2008003707

BRITISH LIBRARY CATALOGUING-IN-PUBLICATION DATA AVAILABLE

Published in 2008 in the U.S. by arrangement with Golden West Literary Agency.
Published in 2008 in the U.K. by arrangement with Golden West Literary Agency.

U.K. Hardcover: 978 1 405 64584 3 (Chivers Large Print)
U.K. Softcover: 978 1 405 64585 0 (Camden Large Print)

Printed in the United States of America
1 2 3 4 5 6 7 12 11 10 09 08

DESERT JOURNEY

1
The Low Desert

Abe Bannion was ten yards ahead of Cal Madison with the waterhole in sight when he reined to a halt and sniffed. There was a scent of wood-smoke. It was very faint but it was there. Abe scratched, swung a searching look all around, decided there had perhaps been someone at the waterhole last night, who had cooked breakfast and pulled out this morning, and eased his big sorrel horse ahead another dozen or so yards, until he could see that the waterhole was deserted.

Abe was greying with that lined, ruddy, weathered look to him a lot of southwestern rangemen had; it made guessing a man's age impossible.

Abe Bannion was average in height, average in build, and even his attire and his riding equipment, were worn and faded and thoroughly nondescript.

When he reached the waterhole and swung

off to instantly begin off-saddling, he glanced around again, and when his partner finally walked his black horse on up and also swung off, Abe said, "No way of telling who he was but he hasn't been gone long." Abe pointed to the black-grey ash, and beside it the smooth imprint of a bedroll.

Cal Madison was a lanky man, roughly Abe's age, sandy-haired, long-faced almost dolorous looking, and had very pale blue eyes. He wore a Colt with an ivory handle, otherwise he was just as faded and nondescript-looking as his partner.

"It's that time of year," he said, working at off-saddling too. "They're comin' up out of Mexico like we did, and they'll be comin' for the next month or more."

They hobbled the horses, washed their backs and left them to pick and choose among the rank grass around the waterhole.

There was a roofless old adobe one-room ruin nearby where some *mestizo* with sheep or goats and not much sense had tried to settle. The walls of the roofless house showed black; some bronco Apache had dropped a fire-arrow on the roof and when the *mestizo* ran out to fling up water, the second arrow had skewered him.

Maybe it hadn't happened exactly like that, but it usually had where riders came upon these forlorn, burnt-out adobe *jacals.*

The Indians, what were left of them, had pulled far back into their mountains. The game of cat-and-mouse they had once played so consistently had ended badly for them. Geronimo, Naná, all that had re-mained of Cochise's band, had been cor-ralled and shipped to Florida and to Indian Territory. The surviving hold-outs no longer raided, they hid and moved at night by stealth. Once in a while a band of them would raid over the line into Mexico, then high-tail back across the border into their mountains, where U.S. troops only half-heartedly searched for them.

The army, like the settlers in Arizona and New Mexico, were of the opinion that Apache raiders up-ending Sonora and Chi-huahua were welcome to that outlet since it kept them too occupied to raid around Ratón or Albuquerque or Douglas, any of the U.S. towns in their path.

An occasional bronco would, however, take to a personal war-trail and it was those warriors men like Abraham Bannion and Caleb Madison were wary about, as they crossed the low desert riding northward towards the far-away hills. In the old days the rag-heads had kept vigils upon every knoll and had allowed no travellers to cross the flat, more or less open desert country without at least being seen. Maybe they weren't still up there watching, and maybe they were; a man wasn't like a cat, when he was likely to have to bet his life on something he couldn't afford to be wrong more than once.

But that hadn't been an Indian who had left his imprint at the waterhole because he had also left some shod-horse imprints and rag-heads rode their horses barefoot.

"Renegade," suggested Cal. "Sure a shame the low desert country's so full of 'em. This time of year they're boilin' up out of Messico where they spent the winter in sunshine, bein' debauched at those Mex *cantinas* and fandango parlours, livin' like lords off their ill-gotten gain."

Abe turned and steadily regarded his partner, and Cal rolled up his eyes in prayerful supplication. "Outlaw, Abe; the bane of the frontier, outlaws and renegades and evil-fellers to a man, and now that the weather is decent again, in springtime and all, those heathens are goin' back up north to practise their malevolent ways."

"Their what?"

Cal smiled. "Malevolent."

"What in hell does that mean?"

"I don't know," replied Cal Madison. "I

10

heard a priest say it at the mission out behind Boca Ratón couple months ago. I think it means something is pretty damned bad."

"Oh. Then why didn't you just say pretty damned bad?"

Cal sighed and changed the subject. "You remember that priest?"

"Father Eusebio Larson?"

"Yeah. Abe, he made the best red wine I ever tasted. While you was over in Texas I'd play checkers and pinochle with him and drink his red wine."

"That's a hell of a name for a grown man," stated Abe, going over to see if he could coax fresh life from the dying embers of that little cooking-fire.

"His real name was Eustace. Eustace Larson," explained Cal Madison. "He used Eusebio because he said it sounded more Mex, and as long as he was serving the church down there . . ." Cal let it trail off as unimportant, and started rolling a cigarette.

From the fire-ring Abe said, "There isn't much choice; Eustace or Eusebio. I wouldn't give a name like that to a lousy biting dog." Abe looked around, but his partner did not seem to be listening as he completed his cigarette and got it lighted, then turned to expansively gaze out over the flat, brushy, ugly vast emptiness they were crossing.

Abe worked at getting the fire burning. It was early afternoon. Too early for supper and too late for dinner, but in the low desert when travellers encountered a sump-spring they pitched camp regardless. Water was all-important and time, especially to the pair camped at the adobe-ruin-spring, meant almost nothing.

Madison strolled over and watched his partner with their fry-pan and coffee pot at the fire-ring. "Two, three more days," he said, through exhaled grey fragrant smoke, and pointed towards the haze-veiled far mountains. "Of course, a feller's got to look a little out. Bad enough all those bad individuals ridin' north this time of year, but there'll be lawmen in the foothills yonder hoping to gather in a few topknots with reward-money on 'em."

Abe looked up, then went on with his cooking without a comment. He, in fact, did not have much to say until they were squatting at the fire eating, and even then his interest seemed limited to the length of time and the route they would use reaching those far foothills. Abe did not like the low desert, but then it would have been very hard to find anyone who did like it — people used it, and always had used it, because it was flat and readily traversible, but generally they did not tarry. Even the mud-wattle Mex villages around the border of the low desert avoided as much contact as possible. There were no towns out in the low desert. There were not even very many old-time abandoned rag-head hideouts. An occasional gutted *jacal* indicated that some-one had once tried to hide out near water, but the stories of what happened to those people was grisly enough without additional embroidery, and if the facts had been known those men had been largely desert-ers from the Mex armies which had once patrolled the low desert. Their lot had been untenable in either case; there were no more cruel officers and edicts than those to be found in *Mejico,* and escape into the low desert was a gamble with very poor odds for survival.

"How many times we made this crossing?" Abe asked, and Cal answered promptly, because he had been wondering the same thing.

"Five, and if we can make it two more years we'll be home free. The priest said so, and he knows law, Mex law and *gringo* law. Seven years is the limit of the statute of limitations."

Abe considered the long, forlorn countenance of his friend. "He sure knew some fine big words anyway, but just the same I'd as leave not put things to the test. Statutes of limitations . . . ?"

"Yeah. That means they can't do anything to fellers who tripped over the law a little after seven years has gone past. I tell you, Abe, Father Eusebio was a clever man — for a reformed horse and cattle thief and gunfighter."

Abe had heard the tales too. They had both spent six months at the village, and excepting three weeks when Abe had gone up into Texas to see a dying relative, they had spent their money at the *cantinas* and the card-rooms and had listened to all the talk, whether it had been in Spanish or English.

"A priest-lawyer," said Abe, picking up his dented coffee cup, "wanted in Texas for a killing, wanted in New Mexico for cattle-rustling, and wanted in Arizona for horse-stealing. Awful busy for a man no older than he looked to be."

Cal chuckled. "How could you tell with all those whiskers covering his face?"

They finished a meagre meal and settled comfortably in the thin shade. It was cool, strangely enough, but then this was early springtime on the low desert, which was actually an extension of cool wintertime because there was little or no change in the vegetation. Elsewhere, springtime brought flowing sap in trees, blossoms and blooms on sage and manzanita and chaparral. On the low desert the scrub-brush, creosote-bush and occasional paloverde came into bloom in the winter after the first rainfall and did not change again for six months, until the last rain was long past and the dry heat had arrived.

There were only two seasons, winter and summer. Winter on the low desert was as balmy and warm and pleasant as most summertimes were at high elevations.

But the land was ugly and treacherous and inhospitable. Abe smoked and leaned with his shoulders upon the high cantle of his saddle, hat tipped down, and considered their surroundings from dead-level grey eyes. The Mexicans had a name for this trip they were making from the border northward across the low desert: *Jornada del muerto.*

Abe turned his head and spat at a fat lizard. The creature gave a scuttling bound and disappeared into the ripgut-grass.

Hell, any trip was a "journey of death" as long as travellers hovered along the border strip where there was very little law and no trust nor faith.

Abe finished his smoke, killed it in the ground at his side, folded both hands over his middle and slept.

Cal strolled forth to watch the horses for a while, then inspected the debris-filled interior of the burnt-out *jacal,* and finally made a circuitous little stroll farther out and around their camp before returning with dusk hovering to drink the last of the coffee and up-end their little pot so it would be dry when Abe made a fresh pot-full.

Cal was a wary man who paced like a lion, Abe seemed to look Fate squarely in the face and make his judgements of everyday reality without much movement and without much noticeable nor audible dissent. They were different in this respect, and also in other respects, but they had been partners for seven years; they complemented each other very well.

As Cal bedded down finally, he listened for strange sounds and eventually fell asleep in spite of himself.

Abe had been snoring an hour before Cal Madison even kicked out of his boots.

2
##
PASO FINO

They rode out early, ahead of the sun, and were up-country a dozen miles before the morning's heat warmed their backs and bones.

It was pure habit; they had both been early-risers since boyhood, but now there was no particular need for straddling leather before dawn; there were no Apaches spying on them and no renegades stalking them. There was not even the low desert heat, which during its proper season was legendary — and deadly.

They had the foothills well within sight as they rode but neither they nor their objective up ahead seemed to be approaching one another very fast. By midday when they halted on the barren flat ridge of a miles deep landswell to make a judgement, those onward inviting hills and mountains looked just as distant as they had looked yesterday.

The desert had air so clear ten miles

seemed less than a hundred yards — until a man tried to ride that hundred yards.

They found an ancient trail which looked to have been brushed off by machete-swinging peons to make way for wheeled vehicles. The historic *caretas* of the Spanish and Mexican south-west, no doubt, since the *gringos* had not owned the low desert when that old trail had been created.

They rode up the old road for a number of miles, and once found a set of adobe buildings, long abandoned and now in a crumbling condition. It had clearly been some kind of outpost — but down in the desert and in an area where the Mexicans had never really made a serious attempt at colonisation because of the deadly Indians?

Cal said, "They had mines up in the mountains. I've heard some pretty tall tales about them, about secret caches of smelted pure gold, and veins in the rock as thick as a man's wrist." As they rode past he gazed at the old buildings. "Corrals, horse-sheds, wagon-houses, a bunk-house and the big one was maybe a sort of counting-house and headquarters."

Abe did not dissent because he agreed; it had probably been a way-station for the pack trains and wagonloads of supplies hauled in, and the gold hauled out.

But the main factor was that the old roadway was still good, and long after Madison and Bannion had lost sight of the ancient structures in their world of empty, golden silence, they still had the roadway.

It skirted low hills and anticipated every arroyo. It remained level completely across the desert, until it suddenly became a forked pathway with a branch heading westerly and the other fork heading easterly, and here the travellers halted to quietly consider the alternatives. Caleb Madison flipped a silver Mex cartwheel; it came down eagle-side up and they turned westward.

The hills which had been so distant for so long, eventually with grudging assent, permitted the pair of horsemen to get close enough to see trees for the first time in several days, and areas of pale, thread-like fine grass. The desert gave way once the foothills were in sight; for a mile or so they merged and created a fragile environment unable to sustain anything which did not graze through and keep going, but farther back where the hills came nearer to the rearward mountains, there was less sign of the desert until in time there was no desert at all unless a man twisted in the saddle and looked back.

By then, the land was richer, the soil

deeper, the graze and browse tougher and more abundant. Here, Nature had cultivated an environment sufficiently varied and virile to support men and animals, even in great numbers, but it had been a generation since people in any numbers at all had been up through these mountains.

Gold, the frontiering argonauts had discovered, was one of those definitely limited resources; it took millions of years to create it, it took a few months to gouge it out, and once it was gone nothing remained in its place but the ravished land.

There had been *peon* miners, then *gringo* miners — the latter infinitely more efficient — and now there was wind in the high pine-tops, sunshine upon the battered land, grass and brush scabbing over the holes and trenches, and silence.

There had once been a town back in the swales and knolls and knobs. It was as deserted now as that way-station mid-way along upon the north-south old roadway leading across the low desert.

The Indians had probably been the first inhabitants of the locale where the village had sprung up, although there was no clear evidence of this now, beyond the clear knowledge that wherever water existed in the south-west, Indians had at one time had villages or at the very least, seasonal camps. But after the *peons* had arrived, a battalion or two of them under Spanish and later Mexican overseers, the customary thick-walled adobe buildings of the south-west arose, and since the mud for the adobe bricks these structures were built out of was mixed from the very earth and water of the immediate area, perhaps old-time Indian artefacts had been included in the bricks.

Not that it mattered. The Mexicans mined for sixty or seventy years, then the south-west passed to the U.S. after the Treaty of Guadalupe Hidalgo, and the next wave of miners arrived, bigger, brawnier, louder, tougher and rougher, more deadly and more efficient. In five years the gold was gone. Improvements created by those *gringos* had been mostly of wood planed and milled from the farther-back forested mountain-sides. It would very often last as long as the earth itself in that dry atmosphere — but not this time.

Some of the *gringos* had remained, had taken up great tracts of land and had turned to cattle-raising. Their homes and barns and sheds and to some extent even their corrals, had been created from the wood hauled away by wagonloads from the forlorn, dead town.

By the time Madison and Bannion reached the outskirts of the lower, rolling country with the desert at their backs and the onward high, deep mountains dead ahead, sunset was nigh and the low, red-gold solemn last rays of the dying day shown upon a few rooftops which had survived the weather, the cattlemen, and even that most mortal of all enemies to man and his works — time.

Abe said, "Well, there she is. No different this year than last year, eh?"

Cal watched the shadows mantle the ghost-town as they approached it, and finally made his judgement. "Too bad it's not near the stageroad. I've seen some sick towns and some dyin' ones, but this here is a dead one and it's too darned bad. A lot of men put a lot of work into making this place."

That was true enough. As they approached the lower, the southern, end of town and the weeds in the ancient roadway slightly impeded their progress, a low little soft warm breeze came down through the completely empty, late-day wide roadway, rattling a few doors, some roof-shakes, and an occasional window-frame. It was as though the skeleton of Paso Fino were uneasily stirring at the arrival in the village of two more *gringos.* It had been those *gringos* who had torn out the gold so fast and had doomed the town. The *peons* who were woefully inefficient, might have mined at Paso Fino for another generation or two. Of course, they brought out only a pittance each year, but then they were not in the hurry the *gringos* had been in.

The source of water for the ghost-town was a well in the central plaza. No Mex town worth the name was without a central plaza and this town, dead or not, was no exception.

The central plaza was a rather circular area with residences, stores, little crooked byways, all converging upon it or facing it. Here, the people, especially the womenfolk, had congregated to fetch water home in earthen jars, to talk and gossip and visit, to do their laundry and to sit endlessly in peaceful shade during the hot summertimes.

The well was encircled by painstakingly meticulous rock-work created by perhaps more than one master-mason and, of course, encircling the flowing spring had raised its water-level. Now, with no one to draw away water, it was even leaking over in several places letting water as blue-green as *anasazi* turquoise go forth across the hushed and empty plaza to water grass and trees and even some inbred rose bushes out back of the adobe church.

When Cal and Abe rode up through town with the echoes of their steel horseshoes making discordant echoes through an endless stillness, the horses scented that spring water. It had been a long while since their last drink so they picked up the gait a little.

There were deer tracks, unshod mustang imprints, even the soft, round pad-marks of cougars at the plaza-spring when Bannion and Madison rode up and dismounted to remove bridles and lead their horses on up.

Neither man drank right away. They leaned across saddle-seats looking around, taking the pulse of the dead stillness, of the hushed and forlorn sleeping old village.

Caleb shook his head. "Always makes me feel like I'm invading someone's grave, riding into this place. It's like a hundred ghosts are standing over yonder among the houses and little stores, watching us. Like they resent us, Abe."

Bannion looked and said nothing until his horse was tanked up and he was ready to lead it away. He might not have said anything even then, but his partner grunted and pointed to a fairly fresh set of shod-horse tracks.

"He's still ahead of us," Abe suggested.

"He's made good time."

There was any number of old empty horse-sheds. The place where Bannion and Madison usually left their horses for the night was in a small pasture surrounded by a stone wall where residue spring-water from the central plaza fanned out and kept the grass nearly stirrup high.

They did not have to forage for horse-feed that way. They led the animals across and out through the nearest clutch of adobe buildings to this stone-walled pasture, and were in fact, off-saddling after glancing in to make certain the feed was as they expected it to be — when a big flea-bit grey horse walked dignifiedly out of some horse-shed shadows across the pasture and steadily approached the men on the far side of the pole-gated stone wall.

Abe Bannion drew in a slow, deep breath, straightened up and very carefully turned half around, looking left and right for the owner of the flea-bit grey.

Cal Madison had his rigging on the ground, had a length of shank-rope in his right hand and was leaning to haul back the gate poles when he saw the grey horse and also slowly straightened up and looked around.

The grey had a washed back which was

the same as having one showing saddle-marks, and there were cheek-piece sweat-stains on his head. The person who had ridden him today had not been off his back very long. Maybe an hour or two but no more than that.

Abe sighed and softly said, "Well, he's here."

"Maybe sleepin' in one of the shacks," said Cal Madison. "Wakin' a stranger out of a sound sleep in a place like this might not be the surest way a man can figure to live forever."

Abe raised his head and whistled. The only immediate attention he got was from the flea-bit grey gelding; he stopped back a few yards and studied Abe with that reproving expression some horses reserved for strangers, especially for strangers who did unpredictable things.

But otherwise there was no response. The echoes departed, the silence came back thicker than ever, and a digger-squirrel poked his head from a hole near the stone fence and angrily chittered at all this needless noise and movement.

Abe looked helplessly at his partner and long-faced Caleb Madison said, "He's got his reasons, Abe. He's got his reasons for not rushing forth and introducing himself.

For all he knows we're a pair of those head-hunting law officers."

Cal did the sensible thing, he led his horse over, lowered the gate-poles and turned his horse into the pasture. The grey watched this with the same disapproving expression but when Cal stood to see if there would be a fight, his black horse was too hungry to be bothered and evidently the grey was not a disagreeable animal.

Abe brought in his sorrel, and he was also too hungry to be immediately concerned about the flea-bit grey. Cal was agreeable when he stepped back to hoist the gate-poles into place.

"Nice animal, nice disposition and nice build . . . Sure never like that colour though."

From back a dozen or so yards in the gloomy layers of mud-wall shade where a harness shop had once been and where now only two glassless windows and a doorless opening looked like eyeless sockets in a weathered dark skull, a man's quiet voice said, "Colour ain't very important, gents. Flea-bit sure enough ain't as pretty as black or sorrel — maybe — but it's the stamina and strength and savvy that a man rides a horse for — not his colour."

They faced around. The stranger was a

man as old as Cal and Abe, perhaps even a day older but it was impossible to be sure, in all those shadows, and he was holding a cocked sixgun casually, but as steadily as stone and it was aimed across at the men by the pole-gate.

"The Lord seen fit to make us in all colours, gents, and in all shapes and sizes, and he left it plumb up to us to figure out the key which would let us know which was true and decent and which was the devil's partners doin' the devil's evil works."

Cal looked at his partner, then over at the man with the cocked pistol. "That's the truth," he warmly conceded, and he even smiled a little, his narrowed eyes reflecting a look which clearly said Cal was convinced they had one of those loners who endlessly rode the low desert, as insane as a pet 'coon, facing them. "The gospel truth, *amigo.*"

The man's wide mouth showed big white teeth when he smiled. He hadn't shaved lately and he was not as tall as Cal although he came close to being like Abe Bannion in size and build. Also, smiling and genial though he seemed now, they both noticed that his sixgun did not waver an inch.

He was amused, obviously, as he regarded Cal and Abe, but seemed most interested in Cal. "Brother, be you a sheep of the Lord?"

he asked.

Cal's head bobbed up and down. "Come from a whole herd of the Lord's lambs," stated the lanky man, and rolled up his eyes heavenward as though seeking someone to bear true witness.

Abe watched this, and snorted as he faced the man with the cocked pistol. "Does your grey horse fight, by any chance?" he asked. "If he does we probably had ought to separate 'em. No sense in getting a horse skinned up in the pasture, *amigo.*"

"He don't fight," stated the smiling man from his shadowy place. "Your's fight, friend?"

"No, neither one of them," replied Abe, eyeing that gunhand and noting with interest how stone-steady it was. Maybe the man could smile and act genial, but that right hand and arm of his weren't all that friendly.

"You been here in Paso Fino long?" Abe asked. "Paso Fino is the name of this place."

The stranger's smile faded a little. "You know how long I've been here, mister. I watched you in the plaza when you saw my shod-horse marks, and before that I watched the pair of you ride up through from the low desert." The gun swung a trifle to cover Abe. "Don't be cute with me, mister!"

29

3
ROBBED!

Nutty as a fruitcake or not the stranger was not one to antagonise as long as he held that cocked Colt. Abe leaned against the stone fence at his back pretending to be a whole lot more casual than he felt, and smiled across at the stranger.

"The shod-marks we saw in the plaza, friend, and I expect if we'd been lookin' for them we'd have seen them back yonder on the trail. But the fact is, we didn't know whether the feller who camped night before last back down where the gutted *jacal* was, came up the east fork or the west fork, and we didn't especially care. You see, we're just on our way through."

The stranger had got a poor initial impression of Abe Bannion, which was unfortunate because those were the impressions which remained with a man.

He turned towards Madison. He had clearly decided that Cal was more nearly his kind of an individual, and Cal who had never been a fool whatever else he had been, had excellent perception; he remained loosely composed and genial. When he said, "We flipped a coin or we wouldn't be here this evening," his idea was to impress upon the man with the gun that he and his partner were not at all concerned with the stranger's presence at Paso Fino. "We been comin' north for quite a few years, mister, but mostly we take the east fork."

The stranger looked doubtful. "Why not this time?"

"Well, like I said, we flipped a coin. And it don't really make a whale of a lot of difference. Easterly, there are some towns, and a good stageroad on through the mountains. Over here, there's a thousand miles of nothing, and if folks aren't in a big rush to get somewhere, it's more peaceful ridin' through from the west of the peaks."

Finally, the stranger eased down the dog and holstered his Colt. He hooked both thumbs and having arrived at some kind of opinion, or decision, said, "I never been up through here before." Then he also said, "Not that I couldn't make it but you boys knowing the way could be a help."

Cal gazed at the man without a word of encouragement and his partner got a slightly vinegary expression on his weathered countenance. They had encountered this sort of thing before; in fact, they had upon several occasions hitched up with another traveller or two, and without exception those relationships had turned out bad.

The stranger gestured. "I got a pan of water ready to boil into coffee out behind the church. You fellers are welcome."

They followed the man. He had a good camp. His bedroll was against the back-wall of the old adobe mission beneath a long, tile-floored rear patio; he could not be caught from in back nor either side. It was a good camp. The kind a man deliberately made up when he preferred not to be surprised.

He even had several armloads of faggots near a hollowed-out place, which had been used for cooking-fires in the rear-yard of the old church for many generations.

They squatted out there while the stranger lighted his shavings and said, "My name is Mortimer," and grinned broadly. "Mort. Folks been calling me Mort since I was big enough to first ride out." He cackled. "You boys know Spanish?"

They "knew" Spanish and Abe guessed why Mortimer had asked: His nickname meant "death" in border-Mex.

"Mort," Abe replied, *"muere, muerto."*

Mortimer laughed and nodded his head vigorously. "My first name is Sampson but no one's called me that since I was a lad. Sampson Mortimer. They been calling me Mort."

Mort Mortimer leaned to blow on the smoking kindling which gave Abe and Cal a chance to exchange a look. Cal rolled up his eyes again but this time with a different meaning.

Abe settled comfortably and fished out his makings to roll a smoke. Mort Mortimer's head came up, his dark eyes watched, then he said, "Brother, that is the devil's weed. Your hands are doing the devil's work."

Abe stopped, gazed at the man in front of him, and debated. It would be easy — and it would also be consistent with his nature — to tell Sampson Mortimer to mind his own damned business. It would also perhaps be wise to establish the boundaries for their relationship at this juncture.

On the other hand Abe did not know how Mort Mortimer might react, and it was after all one cigarette they were bristling about; one cigarette was not important at all. He smiled, tossed aside the troughed paper with

tobacco in it, and put up the sack of tobacco.

Instantly Sampson Mortimer's face
cleared, his expression of geniality returned,
and as he leaned to feed more faggots into
the small fire beneath his coffee-pot he
looked entirely placated.

An hour later, after coffee and a pleasant-
enough visit with their fellow-inhabitant of
Paso Fino, the pair of men from below the
border strolled back in the direction of the
plaza, and this time when Abe started his
smoke he finished it, lighted it, and enjoyed
it as he said, "I figured it would happen
sooner or later . . . Us getting our come-
uppance. Well, you getting it anyway, and
me being there beside you when it happened."

Lanky Cal Madison halted and turned.
"What the hell are you talking about?"

"Remember that time you told me you'd
never been baptised?"

Cal gazed critically at his partner. "Yeah, I
remember. What of it?"

"This is your punishment. Us riding into
that *loco cabeza* back there. That darned
ding-dong. *I* never had anything like this
happen."

Cal stared. "You've never had anything
like . . . You damned idiot you're sounding

34

as crazy as he is."

"Oh, no," exclaimed Abe, exhaling smoke. "It's you, and I got a notion to tell him here you are fifty years old and never been bap—"

"I am not, by gawd, any fifty years old, and you blasted well know it!"

"Well, whatever you are — and you not being baptised and all, you'd ought to be ashamed, Caleb Madison. I'd better tell him. He's bound to be some kind of preacher and he could dunk your head in the well at the plaza and baptise you."

"No one's going to stick my head under no water. I never could stand that."

Abe looked out towards the empty plaza. "Yeah, I know. You're the only feller I ever saw swim a river or take a bath without washing his hair. It's going to make you bald someday, too."

Cal turned off over in the direction of the pole-gate, where they had left their saddle and blankets, their bridles and other personal things. He knew he was being teased but he also knew Abe was capable of carrying his teasing to the point where he would really tell Sampson Mortimer that Cal had never been baptised.

Until now, it had never seemed very important. Cal had always assumed that a lot of men never got baptised. In fact, Cal hardly thought of it, ever. It just was not a very important thing in his life. One drink of water on the low desert was vastly more important.

He mused along and looked up only when Abe swore, stepped past in a hurry and halted above his up-ended saddle. The boot was empty. Cal went over where he could see better and noticed that his carbine boot was also empty.

Abe said, "That crazy bastard somehow slipped down here ahead of us and . . ."

Cal leaned forward, hands on his knees, studying something in the dust near the pole-gate. He ignored his partner until Abe stopped mumbling and walked over, then Cal pointed to a small boot-print. "That," pronounced Cal Madison, "was not made by Sampson Mortimer."

"In'ians got little feet," said Abe, and straightened up to twist and look elsewhere. "Gawddammit, they were watching us when we rode in and when we walked away with . . . Hey, Cal, did you see Mortimer's Winchester hanging in its boot on the post of the veranda behind the church? They didn't bother him, did they?"

Cal straightened up and took his time about answering his partner's angry outburst. "If he led us away so they could steal our carbines, why then I'd say he's our key to getting them back. We may have to knock him black-and-blue though." Cal looked around trying to trace out where those small boot-prints went. He lost sight of them near the wall.

"If that was a rag-head," he opined aloud, "how come him to be walking flat-footed and wearing white man's boots?"

"Stole 'em," snapped Abe. "Stole those boots just like he stole our carbines. Where do the tracks go? I'll hunt that bronco down if it takes all summer."

They tried to pick up the tracks and they were not novices at this, but the best they could do was surmise since the tracks vanished into thin air beside the stone fence, was that the carbine-thief had jumped atop the stone wall and had departed by walking along the top of it.

Abe tapped his partner's shoulder. "Let's go back," he said, and struck out for the rear yard of the old abandoned church.

When they came around the south wall Sampson Mortimer looked up. He had evidently heard them coming. He was smiling a little but he was also standing loosely and facing them. The impression he projected was of a man equally as ready to be a friend or an executioner.

"Fetch back some grub, gents?" he asked. "I figured we could maybe fry up our supper together this evening. A man's got to have associates from time to time. The Good Book says folks got to cleave together one to the other, and such like."

Cal nodded and waited, thumbs in his shellbelt. When Abe moved around to face Sampson Mortimer, Cal was his support. Abe did not look like a man who very often required reinforcements, and when he said, "Mister Mortimer," his voice had a noticeable edge to it.

"Mister Mortimer, when we rode in, we each had a booted carbine. Just now when we got back where we'd left our outfits, the carbines was plumb gone."

Without blinking, Sampson Mortimer offered a little tolerant smile and made a slightly deprecating hand-gesture. "That'll be the lad, I expect, gents. You know how it is, when they're raised up like that."

Abe squinted. "What lad?"

Sampson Mortimer pointed in a general way towards the gentle rolling country northward, but mostly westerly from the ghost-town. "Lives out yonder a couple miles. One time I expect he was a decent boy. He tried to make off with my carbine too, but I figured he was around and I almost caught him. Had his shirt-tail in my grasp, gents, and he wiggled away like a minnow, and he run like a crippled saint with the Devil right ahind him. I never got close."

"How do you know where he lives if you never got close?" Cal asked.

"I got a-horseback, gents, and tracked him out across the range to the ranch, and when I rode up onto the knoll, he was down there in the yard plain as day."

"And you didn't go down?"

"Sure didn't," replied Sampson Mortimer. "He was waitin' down there steady as a log with a big old long-barrelled rifle balanced across the rail fence. Gents, if he was any kind of a shot at all he could have caught me plumb square the moment I commenced riding down off the knoll." Sampson Mortimer smiled. "What would you have done?"

Cal answered. "Turn right square around like you done, Mister Mortimer, and rode away from there."

"Exactly," said the man by the little fire. "Would you gents like to fetch over your supper-stuff and throw it in with mine?"

Abe looked as though he did not especially want to do this, but the look on the stranger's face made him relent. For a fact, there

39

were few more unpleasant things in this life than eating alone.

On the walk back Cal said, "Well, with him there was no reason to ride down there. With us — the lad's got our guns and we're likely to need them before we get far north. You can't do much pot-hunting with a six-gun."

Abe agreed, then he also said, "Mortimer sort of makes me feel like there's something about him . . ."

"Well, hell," stated Cal matter-of-factly, "we already decided he's shy a few beans upstairs."

"No, it's more than that," said Abe. "It's something else."

"Explain," commented Cal, turning towards their saddlery at the pole-gate.

"Just now he was as rational as you or me," answered Abe Bannion. "Other times, he gets as squirrely as an outhouse-mouse. Some of the time when he's talkin' he makes good sense and don't seem wrong at all. Then — like he did when I was fixin' to smoke — he acts crazy as a *pukutsi*-Comanche."

Cal leaned to untie the thongs holding his saddlebags. "Most crazies are like that, aren't they?" he said. "They aren't plumb squirrely all the darned time."

"Well, I don't understand it," mumbled Abe, also pulling loose his saddlebags. "And I don't think I like it very much, neither. But right now I'm more interested in how we're going to get those Winchesters back."

"Easy," said Cal, shouldering his saddlebags. "After full dark we'll ride out there and find that lad, and take back our guns and paddle his doggoned britches . . . Without letting that *pukutsi* named Mort know what we're up to. I don't know how crazy his kind of crazy is; I'd hate like hell to run on to him over there too, and have him get the drop on us again."

They walked back to the mission and around back. Sampson Mortimer had a slightly larger fire going and he beamed when they walked up. His dark eyes studied each of their faces in turn with an intentness he had not showed them before, then he averted his face as they knelt to dig out provisions, and when they later on would have helped, he declined, evidently happy to do the cooking, which would have made him suspect even if Abe and Cal did not already suspect him of being a madman. No rangeman who ever lived and was a tophand at his profession, liked to do camp-cooking.

But Sampson Mortimer was more than a

41

camp-cook. He was the only man Bannion and Madison had ever run across who could make a gravy from baking soda and stringy Mexican beef-jerky, which tasted as though it were the juice of a standing rib roast.

He also made biscuits in the top of a small flour sack which were as light as feathers, but perhaps most interesting of all, while the two stony-faced low desert riders stuffed themselves, Sampson Mortimer beamed. He was clearly very pleased to have diners who would eat.

Later, when they praised his cooking, which in itself was an unheard of occurrence among rangemen, Mortimer said, "I cooked for the General's mess, and most of the time we was in the field, so I had to learn how to make-do a lot of the time and still come up with something the General would eat."

They tactfully tried to draw him out about which General he was referring to, and where he had cooked for the General, but Sampson Mortimer would simply look at them blankly, and change the subject.

Later, using as their excuse the fact that they wanted to go look in on their horses, Abe and Cal left the rear yard of the old church. As they strolled southward down through the silent ghostly village, Abe rolled a smoke and lit it.

Cal said, "He's a friendly cuss."

Abe agreed. "Sort of likeable, but I'll hold up my real opinion until I find out whether he had anything to do with that lad making off with the carbines."

4
A NIGHT FOR RIDING

They rode south-west rather than north-west so that Sampson Mortimer would not hear them leaving town.

They had been up through this area before but never on an excursion; they had simply camped at the ghost-town then had pushed onward, and now as they went quietly out through the settling night the land under stars and a sickle-moon lay open and rolling and very pleasant with lowland oaks and even an occasional cottonwood, trees which were shallow-rooted and lived only where there was water at decent depths.

There was grass for hundreds of cattle, without so much as a single cow anywhere in sight although they encountered a bear from the high country, and this meeting made them both curse because although their saddle-animals were sensible and well-trained, no horse alive could abide the scent of a bear, up close. They had to battle their animals around and onward until the bear-scent was well to the rear, then the horses became tractable again although when they next came upon a half-dozen black-tail deer browsing through some thickets and among some clumps of white oak, the horses shied again, but not as violently, and responded to a good swift kick by straightening out.

Otherwise they met a coursing small band of coyotes. The little sharp-eyed animals must have picked up mounted-man-scent first, though, because they were already scattering when Abe and Cal came up and saw them.

Cal shook his head. "This blasted country's got more inhabitants than a man can shake a stick at."

"But not cattle," grumbled Abe, still annoyed with his horse. "I thought there were cow outfits around here. I'm sure I was told that a couple of years back when I ran onto a couple of horse-stealing rangeriders down over the line. They said this whole country up through here was being taken over by cowmen."

"Not around here," stated Cal, and looped his reins while he rolled and lit a smoke, then retrieved the reins as he studied the stars. They were bearing a little more northward now, and as they held to that route the flatness, the rolling landswells of grassland began to roughen a little, to become slightly steeper and more willing to show rock outcrops.

"Longest two miles in history," Abe dryly said, after they had been more than an hour on the trail.

Cal turned more northerly without comment until they breasted a swale upon the far side of a long thin line of trees, and could distantly make out what looked to be a pale orange glow of steady lamplight. "That's it," he announced. "That's got to be it."

He was right; they had seen no other light and from their point of vantage upon the crest of the low swale they could see in all directions without sighting another building or even another clump of trees where a building could be.

Abe leaned, estimated the distance, then said, "Mort's wrong. Even riding straight from town it's closer to three miles."

They walked their horses prudently and kept the orange lampglow on their right as they circled up-country so as to approach from the direction anyone from Paso Fino would be least expected to appear from, and when they were less than a half mile out, with no trees interfering with night-vision,

Abe raised a thick arm to point.

"House there; looks like more'n a shack too, even at this distance and in that lousy light. Barn yonder. Shoeing-shed or bunkhouse across from the barn." He allowed his arm to drop and spat aside, then said, "Hell, Cal, that's a ranch, that's not some settler-shanty."

"Who said it had to be a shanty?" Madison wanted to know. "All Mort said was that the boy came from a couple miles over in this direction."

Abe reined out and let his horse walk another hundred or so yards, then he swung down, took hobbles from behind the cantle and knelt to fasten them. As he arose and waited for Cal to finish the same operation he scratched under his jacket, made a thoughtful assessment of the onward territory as well as he could make it out, and when they started forward again, on foot, Abe led off and continued to do the guiding.

All he knew was that the boy who had stolen their Winchesters had also anticipated Sampson Mortimer, which meant he was *coyote* enough to anticipate some sort of angry reaction from the two strangers he had stolen the carbines from, and that being true, Abe had no intention of being caught flat-footed twice in the same day, and not when the second time it would amount to being caught by a stripling youth.

He moved northward to get some of those log sheds between himself and Cal, and that solitary lighted window in the front of the main-house on southward across the yard. He utilised every shadow, every inhibiting structure which would conceal the progress of two sturdy men, and when they were close enough he also leaned to craftily study the yard, then utilise the walls and backs of buildings until he was as close as they could get to the main-house.

Here, either by accident or on purpose the man who had organised and erected those ranch-buildings had left a considerable distance between his residence and any of the other buildings.

In the early days that had been deliberate; it had been just one more precaution against being massacred, but judging from the look and feel of the logs used in these structures none of the buildings were more than six or seven years of age.

Not that it mattered how nor why this had been done; what mattered was that it had *been* done and when Abe finally halted to lean and look across at the lighted window of the main-house, he had roughly fifty yards to cross where there was no shelter nor protection of any kind.

If that lad with the rifle was still expecting retaliation, and was over there in the Stygian shadows of the ranchhouse porch . . .

Cal said, "If we split up; one stays here and tries from in front, the other one goes round back and tries from there . . ."

Abe shook his head. Nothing in the world was going to induce him to cross this open space towards the front of that house. He turned to lead off back the way they had come in order to get around upon the opposite side of the yard and work their way on around towards the rear of the house. The lad, if he were lying out there with his blasted rifle, could only watch one direction. The most reasonable direction would be the front where most callers, even nocturnal ones, would appear.

Of course, the odds were roughly even that he could also be around back, but they had to go one way or the other and the rear approach seemed least hazardous so they went around in that direction.

The rear of the house had several comforting elements; one of them was a large wellhouse which was probably also the cooler- and storage-shed, something which was not uncommon among ranch-residences and their utility buildings; if all those things could be combined under one roof it eliminated erecting three separate buildings, and it also kept tinned and bottled goods cool in summertime, as well as providing a cooler-house for the storage of perishables. In this particular case that shed was thick and stout and twice the size of the ordinary well-house, so the pair of men from Paso Fino had no difficulty getting up along the back-wall, which put them quite close to the rear porch of the ranchhouse.

There was no reflection of that parlour-light out back. It was especially dark back there because someone had planted poplar trees only a few years earlier and now they were at least thirty feet tall and thick with their shadows by day as well as by night, darkening the rear of the house.

Cal smiled and nudged Abe. They could reach the rear porch handily. Abe stepped clear and started forward, working his way in and out among the poplars until he was at the west end of the porch. When he vaulted up there, landing cat-footedly without a sound, Cal was leaning just beyond with his sixgun ready.

But there was no one out there; at least no one challenged them. Cal stepped across to the porch-planking and followed his partner as Abe stealthily made his way to the door in the middle of the rear-wall.

It was barred from the inside, which came as no surprise. Abe leaned down, drew forth a boot-knife and felt along the rough wood for the crack between moulding and door. In older houses there had ordinarily been enough shrinkage over the years for a man's knife-blade to ease through and get under the *tranca,* the wooden bar which was set into place in steel stirrups behind a door to lock it from uninvited egress. Not this time; the house was either not old enough for there to be shrinkage, or else the man who had made the moulding and the door had allowed for shrinkage so that now it was impossible to more than insert the tip of the blade.

Abe murmured a curse, sheathed the knife and looked along the wall for a window. There were two, both with solid wooden shutters barred in front of them. Abe tried one window and Cal went to gently examine and probe the other one. Abe was more annoyed than angered when he failed at the window too, and stepped softly over where Cal greeted him with an upraised left hand. With his other hand Cal gently pulled back one of the shutters. He said, "Not latched."

Neither was the window, protected behind

the shutter. Someone had got careless. They could double over a little and step through into Stygian darkness flavoured with the smell of wood-smoke and savoury cooking.

They were inside a bedroom. It was very small with a rather low ceiling. There was a bunk-bed built against a wall and a dresser with a mirror above it. Otherwise there was a clothes-pole and a commode set. There was also a closed door and when Cal leaned to open it very slowly and gently, the warmth from out front reached through to them, along with a strong scent of kitchen-odours.

The corridor was narrow and dark, but reflected lamplight two-thirds of the way along limned a doorway. They tiptoed down in that direction, halted a yard this side of the doorless opening and distinctly heard wood occasionally popping in a fireplace, but that was all for a long while, until a boy's piping voice said, "I'll clean and oil the traps tomorrow and hang them in the barn-loft . . . We have two bales, and that's better'n we had last year, maw."

For a while there was no answer. The fire popped and someone steadily rocking in a chair were the only sounds, then a softer and deeper voice said, "Two bales ought to help us through — if we can put down enough food this summer." The voice belonged to a woman and it lacked timbre, or depth. It was a pleasant voice but it seemed to reflect something close to either dejection or resignation, or perhaps illness. From where the men from Paso Fino stood the only distinctive factor seemed to be the lack of inflection; the sound of someone talking without thinking about what they were saying. A definitely flat sound.

"This summer we'll have plenty of meat to put down," the lad's voice said, firming up into almost a boasting tone.

Cal nudged his partner and jutted his jaw in a gesture to advance. Abe moved up to the doorway, leaned to look around into the lamplit parlour with its glowing hearth, and did not pull back until he located a long-barrelled rifle on antlers above the mantle, a carbine leaning beside the jam of the front door, and a holstered Colt with a carved walnut handle hanging from a hat-rack across the room, also by the front door.

He could not see the woman, except that she had black hair and had her back to him in the rocking chair, but the boy was over in front of the fireplace standing like a man, wide-legged, arms behind him to the warmth, with a tousled head of taffy hair and a lanky, lean look to him.

Abe sighed, reached for his Colt and without a sound stepped into plain sight. Cal walked out behind him, but Cal did not draw his gun. He did not have to; there was only an unarmed boy and a black-haired woman crocheting in a rocking chair, neither of them within lunging distance of a weapon.

For five seconds the boy did not notice movement where a tall lanky man and a shorter, thicker man walked slowly and very carefully forward. Then he saw them — and turned to stone!

They were behind the woman, big-looking, villainous in the shifting weak lamplight, one with a sixgun aimed towards the boy, as menacing as two unexpected men could possibly look.

The boy seemed completely paralysed.

5
ADVENTURES!

She murmured something to her son about another log on the fire, and when he did not move she raised dark eyes.

For a moment she stared, then she leaned and almost methodically lay aside her crocheting, picked up the little wicker basket she apparently kept her darning and crocheting implements in, and twisted around in the chair to look behind her.

She had one hand in the little wicker lap-basket. She sat like that, twisted, her right hand out of sight, dark, large eyes fixed on Abe and Cal, then she spoke in a perfectly normal voice.

"You won't find anything here worth stealing. We don't even own a good horse any more."

Cal stepped around, moved over and smiled as he gently took the little wicker basket, stepped back and felt inside it. There was an under-and-over .41 derringer beneath the yarn and implements. It had an ivory handle. Cal examined it, made a little clucking sound of disapproval, and dropped the derringer into his coat pocket.

Abe holstered his Colt. "Your name, ma'am?" he asked. "And the boy's name?"

She answered in the same calm tone. "I am Sylvia Weatherby. That is Sandringham Weatherby, my son."

Abe considered the woman's face. She was very handsome but in a way he could not quite define — haunting, hurt, painful, humbled way. He tried to fit a word and none fit. He raised his head a little to the boy, thinking a boy's folks had to be hard up for a name to hang something like Sandringham on a lad.

"Sandringham," he said, pronouncing it slowly in order to get it right. "You got an idea who we are and why we're here tonight?"

The boy was white to the hairline. His eyes left Abe only to watch Cal find his mother's little derringer, then he looked back at Abe, who happened to have been the first one of them he had seen and who also happened to be the one with a gun in his hand when Sandringham had first seen him.

This had to be Abe Bannion's day for not

making very good first impressions.

"Did you hear me, lad?" Abe said.

The woman turned slowly from watching Cal. She gazed in the direction of the fireplace. "Sandy . . . ?"

The boy locked fists and stiffened where he stood, forcing defiance to replace the shock, the fright and astonishment which had held him soundless until this moment. "Maw, they're more saddle-bums camping over in Paso Fino. They just rode in today, when I was hauling in the last of the trapline in the willows out behind the church. There is another feller, but he came in yesterday." Sandringham Weatherby looked from his mother to Cal Madison. "That skinny, long-legged one was riding a black horse and this old-looking, shorter one was riding a sorrel."

Cal squinted at the lad, and leaned to put aside the darning basket. "If I was named Sandringham, I wouldn't be too darned critical of other folks, son," he said, "and for your information, I'm not skinny, I just grew too fast when I was your age . . . Sandringham, want me to tell your maw why we're here?"

The lad's colour returned and steadily increased until he was red in the face. His mother noticed. She turned towards Cal.

"You should be proud; you've managed to frighten a child."

Cal looked down. She was an uncommonly handsome woman. "Where is your husband?" he asked, and got a curt answer.

"My husband is dead . . . Two years ago this spring."

Cal digested that, along with its implications, and raised a hand to his scratchy jaw as he glanced back towards the fireplace. "Well, sir, boy, do like your maw said — put another log on the fire!"

Abe moved around where he could see the woman and where she could see both Abe and Cal without sitting awkwardly twisted in the rocker. He soberly watched the lad go to the wall woodbox, balance a thick round of pine with one hand while he closed and latched the woodbox door with the other hand, then go to the wide, deep maw of the stonework fireplace and put on the log. As the boy straightened up turning back Abe said, "Does that rifle over the door fire?"

The boy flicked a glance up there. "Yes, sir, it'll shoot."

"And that Winchester carbine beside the door — will it also fire?"

"Yes, sir."

Abe studied the lad's features for a moment before saying, "Then will you tell me why in hell — excuse me, ma'm — you had to steal two more carbines?"

For a moment the room was silent enough for its inhabitants to have heard a pin drop. Even the fireplace did not pop. Then the boy shot a sidewards glance at his mother, and she sat there erectly in her rocking chair, hands in her lap, looking with dark-eyed solemnity back at her son.

"I — needed them," he finally said.

Abe shook his head. "Naw, I don't believe that, boy. If you already got two long-guns that'll fire . . . Boy, you can't shoot but one carbine at a time."

Cal said, "Come on, Sandy; stealin' the guns was bad enough, don't make us dislike you any more by lyin'. You know, there's nothing worse than a liar, son."

Sylvia Weatherby shot a flashing dark look at Cal but said nothing. Not until she was again facing her son, then she spoke in her soft, deep-toned way and the boy's attention went to her instantly.

"Did you take their carbines, Sandy? Why, I want to know, and I think they deserve to know too . . . Sandy?"

"I figured to trade them the next time a band of In'ians came through. Get three, maybe four, horses for us, maw. We need horses bad and you know it, and there's no other way for us to get 'em." The boy pushed his words out almost all together, and afterwards he stood breathing a little harder than before.

Abe picked off his hat, turned and flung it upon a leather sofa, then he shot Cal a glance and turned to step over, with his thick back and oaken legs to the fire. The lad was a yard away on Abe's right side. In comparison, it was like an oak and a sapling.

"You folks are alone out here?" Abe asked the handsome woman. "Lady, I'm not prying and I'm not asking so's my partner and me can raid you."

"Then why do you ask at all?" the woman asked, in a very sweet voice, and she smiled in a way that normally would have made Abe stop dead still then and there. "Sandy will return your guns, and I'll apologise for what he did and for causing you all the inconvenience. I'd offer to pay you but we don't have any money."

Cal fished out the ivory-gripped derringer, broke it, extracted both cartridges and dropped it back atop the things in the wicker basket, then he stepped to the door and looked out around the dark yard, closed the door and set his back to it as his eyes and the eyes of the tall boy met.

Abe said, "You had horses and cattle, missus?"

She answered flatly, in that same dull voice he had first heard her use. "Yes, we had some cattle, and we also had a team, four saddle animals and a milk cow." She looked up again. "The teams went first, then the milk cow, and finally the saddle horses, one at a time."

Cal said, "Branded, was they, missus?"

"Yes. Circle W. A large rib-brand; a big circle with the letter W inside the circle." She made a little gesture. "My husband used to say that someday the law would come in here and clean this country out, and down along the border as well, then decent folks would be able to improve their herds and build up their ranches . . ."

Abe looked back at the fire. That log was robustly burning; he had to move forward a foot. "Your husband died?" he asked, encouraging the woman to speak on this subject.

"Stomach bile," she said. "One day he got sick and two days later he was dead, poisoned by the stomach bile."

Abe understood this by another name, but he had heard it called "stomach bile" before. Appendicitis. Ruptured appendix. He gathered himself together and turned.

"Sandy, fetch in our carbines."

The boy turned without a word and walked out of the warm and lighted parlour. His mother considered the little empty derringer atop the things in her sewing basket. "I want to make it right," she said quietly, in that flat tone of voice. "I only have him." She turned towards Abe. "I'm not begging for him, mister, I'm just asking that whatever you do, you remember I don't have anyone left but him."

Abe moved uncomfortably, shot his partner a look, then said a trifle gruffly, "We're not going to do anything, missus. But you'd ought to make him understand that stealin' could get him shot and killed someday . . . I understand why he did it . . . I grew up sort of like he's doing . . ."

Cal rubbed his bristly jaw. "That was an awful long while ago, though."

Abe glared. "By gawd, at least I was baptised! Missus Weatherby —"

The lanky boy returned from the back of the house with a Winchester saddlegun under each arm. He mutely handed them to Abe who in turn tossed one to his partner. Then Abe stood holding his carbine in the crook of an arm eyeing the tall youth. He did not smile; did not, in fact, even look very grateful as he spoke harshly.

"You got two bales of furs; why can't you trade them to the tomahawks for horses?"

"They got all the hides they want, mister, and besides they're better trappers and skinners than I am. They wouldn't trade for my plews — but they'll take guns. I know, because a couple of times when I've met bands on the move and they've seen my rifle, they've offered horses in trade."

The boy looked steadily at Abe. He was as tall but only about a third as thick and powerful. Youth had its advantages, clearly, but under some circumstances they were nowhere nearly as valuable as the altogether different kind of advantages that went with a man's prime age.

"I'm sorry I took your guns," the boy said to Abe, without lowering his eyes. "I knew it was wrong . . . I just figured . . . I see men ride into the old ghost-town pretty often this time of year, and I reckon most of them are outlaws running from the law, or something like that, and I figured you would be doing the same and that you wouldn't want to take the time to try and find who took your guns." The boy's hands fluttered a little at his sides. "I — already said I'm sorry, didn't I?"

Abe nodded. "Yeah, you already said that." He came near to smiling. "Don't steal, boy. Not for your maw's sake or mine or anyone else's but your own sake. Boy, don't lie and don't steal and if you make a point in life of not lettin' yourself get into situations where you're going to have to do one or the other, you'll make out better than most men." He turned and crossed to the door, turned back and smiled, finally, at the handsome dark-eyed woman, then he nudged Cal and they left the house by the front door.

By the time they got back to the horses, pulled off the hobbles and were ready to return to Paso Fino they had both digested all they had heard back at the ranch, and had made a few judgements as well.

"Darned woman had ought to sell out if she can and head for a town," was Cal Madison's opinion, and his partner did not entirely dissent, although it did not seem to him she would be able to sell.

"At least, not for enough to get her very far away. Who'd buy? As near as we've seen, except for a bear now and then, some grouse maybe and coyotes, who lives out in here?"

It was a good point. Cal nodded over it and set their course directly overland to the ghost-town. He yawned a couple of times and by the end of their ride he was ready to turn the horse into that little stone-fenced pasture and hunt up his bedroll.

There was not a sound through the empty village. The only indication that Sampson Mortimer was around was the smoke-scent still in the air.

As Cal kicked out of his boots, looped his gunbelt and put it beside his bedroll, he said, "Darned monkey business anyway," and vigorously scratched as he eased down upon the worn old groundcloth-canvas.

They had their camp, such as it was, beside the pole-gate with their saddlery, the retrieved Winchesters, their boots and other effects within reach. It was the night-camp of men who wanted everything handy for the darkness before dawn when they would rig out and start up the trail again, early.

Abe sighed, looked over, saw Cal's lumpiness and said, "Poor damned kid, anyway."

"Go to sleep, darn it . . . What a hell of a long day this one's been!"

It wasn't quite finished yet.

"Evenin', gents," the genial voice called ahead through darkness as Sampson Mortimer approached. "Hope you don't mind a friend droppin' in to visit a spell."

Abe raised only his head, like a turtle, eyed the visitor with a jaundiced expression, and when Cal sat up, yawned and said, "Come right on in; hell, don't neither of us need much sleep anyhow," Abe swore, twisted inside the warming bedroll and also sat up.

Sampson Mortimer walked up, found no coals to hunker by, and went to lean upon the stone-fence and make himself a cigarette. "I see you got 'em back," he murmured, gesturing towards the carbines in their scabbards. "You must've weaselled around over their pretty good, for that blasted boy's a wary one."

"It was dark," explained Cal, rubbing his eyes. "We slunk around back." He blinked rapidly and watched Mortimer light his smoke.

"Quite an outfit, though," said Mortimer. "I set up there admirin' those log buildings. You know, gents, a man'd have to work like a slave for a long while to erect a house and barn and them what-not buildings like that."

Abe and Cal studied Mortimer trying to guess what lay in his mind. Abe finally said, "Are you a rancher, by some chance; maybe a cowman, Mister Mortimer?"

"Oh, hell," chuckled the smoking man. "Why'n't you boys just call me Mort." The chuckle deepened a little. "Death, boys; just call me death."

Abe did not laugh and his partner sat and

narrowly studied the man over against the fence.

"Naw," stated Mortimer. "I'm no cow-man. Haven't worked out of a cow-camp since I was in my twenties. For a fact, though, years back I rode and worked the ranges. It's a miserable life, boys, the pay is bad, the hours is impossible, the work is terrible hard, and there's no future. The Lord came to me one Saturday night in a saloon where there'd just been a bad fight; He came to me and brought me to the light, gents, and ever since then I been His true instrument."

Cal made a weak little smile. "Well, I reckon a man could sure work for a worse range-boss."

"Halleluleh!" exclaimed Mortimer, and gestured with his cigarette. "You boys is on the road to becomin' one of the Lord's lambs. I can sense it in the night around us."

Abe yawned widely. The only thing he could sense in the night was that if Sampson Mortimer didn't give up pretty quick and go on back to his own camp, Abe was going to fall asleep and snore and embarrass all three of them.

Mortimer suddenly smiled at Abe and said, "Good night, brother. I just wanted to make plumb sure you got back all right. I figured where you'd gone the minute you left my camp a while back. Well, see you in the morning, gents. We'll have stewed plums."

They sat and watched him walk up the empty, haunted old dusty roadway in the direction of the church. It dawned on Cal why Sampson Mortimer had made his camp at the old mission.

"What's a feller like that do when he's got to camp where there isn't any church?" Cal asked, and Abe, already easing back down under the blankets, made a dry reply.

"Probably makes his camp in the cemetery. Shut up and go to sleep, will you? If he hears us talkin' he might come back."

Cal, who had been so tired a short while before was now fully awake. "Stewed plums for breakfast? Where in hell would he get something like that?"

"Maybe he's the sugar-plum fairy," Abe growled from inside his mounded blankets. "If you don't shut up . . ."

Cal got down, too, grumbled under his breath and threshed until he was fully comfortable, then he also composed himself for sleep.

It was a pleasant night, chilly at times and just ahead of dawn it got downright cold with the temperature fluctuating around freezing.

There was a high, long veil of pale cloudiness stretching almost from horizon to horizon, but it was not visible until first-light, and even then because it was so vaporous — and also because Bannion and Madison had a fresh interest to hold their attention — the pale cloudiness went pretty much unnoticed.

Paso Fino had been awakening to this kind of a soft-rose dawn for more generations than anyone really knew, and it was just as silent, as shadowily forlorn and endlessly hushed as it had been all those other mornings.

A few animals had come in the night to drink at the central plaza, and to instantly depart because the scent of Man was strong; excepting their tracks, though, there was no indication that in the night the town had not been as empty as it might have seemed.

Abe arose, looked off to his right in the direction of the plaza, then reached for his hat which he crushed down over the awry hair, reached for his boots and after tugging them on, he arose to yawn, to expectorate, and to vigorously scratch as he turned to his right to gaze at the big, lanky lump under those blankets and that square of old, stained canvas. Cal was snoring, but softly, like a shoat caught under a fence.

Abe grinned and raised his eyes. There was dew on the grass beyond the stone fence, far off the eastern sky was changing soft shades from moment to moment . . . He slowly brought his attention back to the dewy grass inside the stone fence.

The horses were gone!

6
TROUBLE!

Cal hurt his big toe on a stone when he jumped out of bed at Abe's profane announcement, and stepped swiftly across to the pole-gate to look around the pasture. He lifted the foot and profanely clung to it while he looked at the big empty field with fresh dawn-light upon it.

"That kid," groaned Cal, working his painful big toe up and down to ascertain that the injury had not been serious. "He likely followed us back last night, and after we went to sleep he stole the horses!"

Abe had noticed something else. The flea-bit grey gelding was also gone, which meant that Sampson Mortimer was also on foot. He said, "Get dressed, I'll go roust out the darned *pukutsi*."

Abe strode briskly through the cold morning air. Around him Paso Fino was beginning to assume shape and depth and new-day colour. When he reached the church and hurried around back, Sampson Mortimer was not there. Neither was his camp; the bedroll, the scattered other camp-gear, all the saddlery, additional equipment, was gone. Abe went to the fire-ring and shoved in his hand. The coals were as cold as stones.

He straightened up and studied the ground until he located shod-horse sign. Mort had ridden out northward, but up at the northern end of the village where there was a stone ledge, Abe lost the sign. Not that he cared right at this moment; he hastened back to his partner and reported. Cal listened, exhaled smoke from the cigarette he was having for breakfast, then jerked a thumb over his shoulder.

"Whoever took our livestock got 'em out through a break in the stone fence on the far side. This time, the bootprints don't belong to any youngster. That feller had feet as big as mine. Run-over on the outside, both boots, and as big as mine."

Abe screwed up his face. He had seen dozens of imprints behind the church and Sampson Mortimer had not possessed big feet. "Show me," he said to Cal, and was led across through the pasture to the deliberate break where someone had very carefully taken down a rock at a time in the night in order to have a way to lead the stolen horses out.

Abe studied the tracks then said, "It wasn't the *pukutsi*, Cal."

"What the hell are you talking about? Who else was around here? Him or Sandringham . . . That's one hell of a name. Anyway, those two or no one."

Abe straightened. "You saw the lad's tracks. These don't belong to him. Go up to the backyard of the church if you got to, and look at those tracks up there. Too small for Mortimer to have made these here tracks. And there's something else: I got no idea why Mort pulled out in the night, but with a feller like him maybe anything is possible, but I *do* know that when he rode out he rode alone — he wasn't leading no additional livestock — so that means there was a third feller around here last night." Abe turned back to the fresh-lighted marks around the broken wall. "Did you track the horses?" he asked, and moved off as though he intended to do this.

Cal had already circled around somewhat. "It's going to take longer legs than we got to follow 'em very far," he called to Abe. "I followed them out half a mile and they were still going." He raised an arm. "That way; up towards the darned mountains. By now I'd guess that horse-thief's five, six miles

73

ahead and still going." Cal gazed for a long moment at the northward mountains; they stopped being foothills about a mile onward and became jagged, steep, rugged terraces of endless uphill hardship. He swore with considerable feeling. "We're not going to overtake that feller, without being on horseback when we do it, Abe."

What especially troubled them as they went back to their saddlebags to munch a cold breakfast, was where the horse-thief had come from, where he might have camped the previous night, and if he'd perhaps left an exhausted saddlehorse back there.

Neither of them acted enthusiastic about making a chase out of what had to be done, but neither did either one of them act as though he were resigned to the loss, and to the increasing probability that they might never recover their horses.

There was also a minor mystery. Since Mort had invited them to breakfast this morning, he had clearly not meant to depart in the night. Why then had he done so?

"Heard someone," suggested Abe. "Heard a rider maybe or another stranger other than us, and decided to leave." Abe shrugged. "Maybe he's a wanted man, but he wouldn't have to be; no one in his right mind would stay in that damned haunted village a minute longer'n he had to, and I wish to hell we'd taken the east fork in the road."

Cal rolled a smoke thoughtfully. "He heard us, or saw us, yesterday, and he didn't run. Why would he run last night, from someone ridin' up?"

"Ask him," granted Abe, wiping his mouth with the back of his hand, and swung his head sharply because he had thought he had caught a very brief glimpse of movement across the plaza.

"And the last I see of this damned town the happier I'll be," he growled, peering intently across among the distant shadows where doorless and windowless Mex adobe huts and shops stood close-spaced and evidently ageless. In a much lower tone he also said, "Cal, there's someone yonder across the plaza on the opposite side. I just caught a glimpse of him."

Cal lighted his smoke, examined the red tip and inhaled, exhaled, and slowly arose to his lanky full height without acting as though he had heard Abe. He blew smoke, studied the far-distant southward low desert, which looked invitingly peaceful and pleasant this early in the morning, and as he stood like this he said, "What do you want to do?"

Abe answered as he turned elaborately to kneel and begin cleaning up after their meal. "I'll stay here and pretend to be busy. You go northward up behind the stone fence and when you get as far as the church, try and duck over across the road. If you can come in behind him . . ."

Cal said, "All right," and without more discussion he returned to the empty pasture by the gateway and moments later he was out of sight in the tall, rank grass.

Abe whistled softly and got their camp in order. He made no move to enter the gateway after his partner nor did he act as though the loss of horses was a particular disaster — which it most certainly was.

Eventually, when it would have been apparent to anyone that he was killing time, he arose with the camp in perfect order, turned and walked out to the centre of the plaza where the spring was, and washed his hands and face, wet down his hair and combed it, then stood a moment examining all the little fresh tracks roundabout before shooting a slowly casual look in the direction he had formerly caught that glimpse of human movement.

There was no additional movement and as close as he could tell, excluding some of the deeper and darker shadowy places, there was no silhouette of a man over yonder.

He started on across the plaza hoping to hold someone's attention as long as he could, paused just short of the plaza's far side to roll a cigarette and light it, then, trickling smoke, he stepped to a doorway and looked inside a shop where a foot of rubble was all that remained of what may once have been a flourishing small business.

Cal called. "Got him, Abe!"

It took another couple of minutes for Cal to emerge through the maze of little Mextown byways into the plaza where his partner leaned, smoking and waiting.

Abe looked, grunted under his breath and walked on up where Cal had a fisted grip on the thin shoulder of the same "bandit" who had raided their camp the previous day, Sandringham Weatherby.

The boy was red-faced and stiff with indignation as he tried one last time to pull free of the powerful grip, and failed.

Abe stopped close and looked disgustedly at the youth. "You sure try a feller's patience, boy; where are the horses?"

The youth glared. "I didn't take your horses!"

Abe said, "Sure not. You just naturally get up ahead of dawn and run two, three miles to get over to this darned town so's you can stand around and spy on folks."

"No, sir, I don't do anything like that. Well, I get up early. I do that every morning because now that we don't have the horses any more, if I'm going to hunt I've got to be out there and in place before the sun —"

"Boy," interrupted Abe severely, "where are our horses?"

Sandringham Weatherby tentatively tried to wiggle out of Cal's grip again, and this time Cal released him. The boy stepped clear and straightened his shirt as he said, "I told you, mister, I didn't have anything to do with that . . . But I know who did, and I know where he's going with your horses."

Abe studied the youth's face. So did Cal. "Spit it out," said the taller man.

"I don't know his name but he's been hiding in an old In'ian cave up through the hills for a couple of months. I've lain atop flat rocks and watched him, and sometimes I've tracked an' trailed him. He's a dark, whiskered feller, about your size," the pointed hand signified Abe Bannion. "He had a horse but it died. I know where he piled stones atop it, too. He's *coyote;* never goes out of the cave if he don't have to, and hunts without using his guns. With snares and such-like."

Abe pulled at his chin. He gazed at the lad without being able to completely conceal the doubt and scepticism he felt. "How do you know he got our horses?" he asked the lad.

"Yesterday, when I was heading home after stealing your carbines, I saw him circling out and around. He was watching that fire the other man made. Up behind the mission church. He was trying to get down close enough to spy on that feller."

Cal stepped to an upright-post and leaned. "If you're lyin', this time boy I'm going to half skin you alive." He gestured. "You lead us to this renegade's hideout, and boy, don't you do anything to let him know we're coming."

Abe, speaking in a way to extract some of the sting from what his partner had said, was less menacing. "All we want, Sandy, is to get back the horses and get the hell out of this crazy blasted place, and I'll tell you what we'll do. You get us up to this darned horsethief and after his hash is settled, if he's got a carbine you can have it to trade to the In'ians for a couple horses. You agreeable?"

The boy nodded. He did not smile because his first fear of these two men had been reserved for this one, the stocky one.

Nevertheless he was pleased. As he turned to lead off he said, "Mister," to Cal Madison. "My mother'd have a plumb fit. She's told me a dozen times not to go anywhere near that man's cave."

"We'll try and set things to right with her," stated Cal, and smiled a little. "Now don't get too far ahead, son, because aren't neither me nor my partner built for walking. Especially in the blasted mountains."

The boy led out with a swinging, long-legged gait which had Cal, who was also tall, stretching his stride, and which had Abe Bannion cursing under his breath all the way to their first halt.

The boy knew his foothills and he also knew as much of the onward mountains as they would cover this morning. He was a natural scout. Without having been taught the ways of stealth and prudence, he had evolved his own techniques and they were excellent.

Once, where the men called a halt, near a little white-water creek, the boy showed them where he had shot a large bear the previous winter. They could tell by the expression on his face at this recollection that he had been terrified. With good reason; any man on foot who hunted bears with a single-shot musket, and was not afraid for his life, was crazier than Sampson Mortimer!

They went straight at a forested slope and when Abe called out pantingly the lad stopped to explain why he had chosen this rougher course.

"Because that renegade don't come over this far to the west, and we got to parallel him or we're never going to get up there in time." The boy looked soberly at Abe. "Mister, there's been other fellers pass through the village and he never came down before to try and steal anything from them, least of all their livestock; mister, I believe that if he'd steal your horses last night it's because he's finally ready to leave the country. Let's get on up there."

Cal and Abe had no chance to confer. Not that a conference was necessary. What the lad had deduced had been about the same thing Abe and Cal had wondered about, because people did not steal horses in isolated places like this unless they had a use for them, and unless they anticipated using them.

The forest was noticeably cooler than it had been back down at the ghost-town. In fact, in some places, canyons and arroyos they crossed where the sun never reached at all, it was downright cold even though it was mid-morning by the time they got roughly half-way to their objective.

The lad never tired, but then, boys his age rarely ever did tire. When Abe asked how much farther, the boy smiled at Abe for the first time, and it tickled Cal because that smile had been one of superiority. Maybe the number of things Sandy Weatherby could accomplish were negligible in contrast to the things Abe Bannion could accomplish, but when one of those rare things occurred — like trotting up the side of a forested mountain — the lad knew it and was bolstered by the knowledge.

"Another mile is all," he said to Abe, and slackened speed a little.

They finally came to a levelling of the slope, and to a place where in eons past something like an enormous ice-field had moved down across a granite mountaintop to completely carry away the upper several hundred yards, and what now remained was a rather dished-out place which, with the depositing of dust and dirt over the millennia, had become an upland, secret meadow. Out about a third of the way from the encircling forest, near where a creek ran through the meadow, was a half-domed great black ledge of rock. Up the far front of the rock was a black stain. This was the tell-tale sign which helped the spying, breathless men from Paso Fino to locate the prehistoric Indian cave.

But more importantly, they saw their horses! The black and the sorrel! They were grazing as contentedly as though they had not been stolen.

Sandy wanted to take them on around to their left, which would put them in a better position to study the cave-front, but Cal reached, caught the lad's arm and pulled him down into the underbrush, where the two men were studying the onward lie of land.

"You did your part and you did it right well," Cal told the lad. "From here on my partner and I'll sort of do the figuring and scheming so you just rest easy now, as the Messicans say, and wait for us to get you that carbine." Cal looked around. "Any objections?"

He smiled.

The youth looked at Cal with fresh interest and smiled as he shook his head. "No, sir, no objections."

Abe had completed his initial examination of the area. What he wanted was a fair sighting of the horse-thief. There was no way to cross that meadow unless a man went the full distance like a snake on his belly, without being seen the moment he stepped from the trees.

Abe sank into a sitting position in the forest-shade and asked about the cave, but the boy had never ventured out there upon the meadow, and therefore had never got close to the cave, so he could volunteer no real information.

It was Cal's opinion that they should lie there and when the horse-thief emerged, shoot him on sight. It was perfectly lawful to do that to a horse-thief; it was a lot more tidy than draping a rope round his neck and leading the horse out from under him.

Abe did not agree nor disagree but he cocked an eye at the sun's location as though to estimate how much time they had left.

It was barely noon so they had plenty of time. Providing of course, the renegade did not decline to leave the cave — providing he was even in there.

Abe composed himself. So did Cal. But the youth fidgeted. He suggested crawling through the grass. They told him that even if they agreed and crawled, he would not be allowed to accompany them. He also offered to lead them around into a position where they would be able to see part way down into the cave as long as the sunlight was in a proper position.

They also declined that offer. Finally, Abe turned with some exasperation and said, "Boy, just set down and be still. When that feller comes back where those horses are, we'll look after him, and there's no point in taking risks when you don't have to."

Sandy sank down, subdued but not happily so and turned from Abe to Cal. Madison ruefully nodded in agreement with what his partner had said, and the boy accepted this nod much more readily. He had evidently decided that he liked lanky Cal and did not especially like stocky Abe Bannion.

7

THE STRANGER

It was a long wait, and when they finally detected movement it was the lad who saw it first and who reached to brush Cal's arm and point.

A man was crossing the meadow but not by walking directly towards the cave even though that seemed to be his eventual destination. He made his weaving way back and forth through the lowest border of tall trees, peering intently at the indifferent horses out there, beyond them in the direction of the cave. It was impossible to tell from that distance but it seemed to Abe that the man was neither a young man, that is he was not in his twenties or his late teens, and it also seemed to Abe that he was compact and thick, like an Apache, but light on his feet and as wary as a wolf.

He had reason to be wary; he would know exactly the penalty for stealing horses, and now as he returned towards the cave he would have reason to worry. He probably did not believe the pair of men on foot back down at the ghost-town could possibly have tracked him this far so soon, and as a matter of fact if they had relied entirely upon tracks they would in all probability not have found the meadow at all because the horse-thief had ridden Abe's sorrel, had led Cal's black, and had ridden in the exact opposite direction from the meadow until he had reached a stone ledge he knew of, and there, where even steel horseshoes did not make an impression, he had turned in a different direction.

He was not a novice, except that he had either not known about the Weatherby lad or else he had not thought the Weatherby lad knew about him. Now, as he came on around the encircling forest until he was fairly close to his cave, Abe finally hit upon a plan. When the stranger was south-westerly he would be actually on the far side of the black ledge of stone where the cave was. In fact, that ledge of stone would not only hide him from the men watching his advance but it would also hide them from him.

Abe leaned. "As soon as he can't see over here I'm going to get as close as I can, and drop down in the grass so when he walks around to the front of the cliff-face I can drop him."

Cal nodded approval but the youth pulled back a little and stared at Abe. Neither of the older men noticed; they were far more interested in the elusive stocky shadow over yonder. To Sandy Weatherby, Abe's cold-blooded announcement that he would drop the horse-thief was a blow. He did nothing and he said nothing, but his colour faded and he did not take his eyes off Abe, whom he now had reason to think of as a cold-blooded killer.

Cal said, "Now," and Abe arose to trot ahead. He ran out of the trees into the clinging, tough meadow grass, and had to exert greater pressure to thrust onward in any kind of haste.

He was exposed but even if the stranger had seen him he might not have made a very good target because he did not run in a direct line.

There was no way for him to reach the cliff-front before the stranger emerged around the side of the cliff-face and he knew it, so when he was close enough, he paused, sank to one knee breathing hard, palmed his sixgun and waited for sounds.

When they eventually arrived it was clear that the stranger was moving with more confidence than he had a right to feel. He made no attempt to be quiet, which might have been difficult in any case since most of the way around the cliff-face was covered for approximately fifty yards out from the front of the rock ledge with an age-old accumulation of stone chips, perhaps flaked away like that by frost and thaws.

There was no such accumulation upon the south slope; there was underbrush there, and trees with fairly deep soil; perhaps if the stranger had considered it possible someone might have been around front listening for him he would have used that more southerly approach.

He came around the rock ledge with a thrusting stride. Now that he was no longer in among trees he was clearly hurrying, and that, of course, added to the normal sounds he would have made.

Abe cocked his Colt, sank down until nothing more of him was visible but the crown of his hat through the tallest stalks and his upper face.

The stranger appeared in full view, and assisted Abe by pausing out there where he had a good view, to range a long, searching look around.

Cal was back there, intently watching from hiding with the lanky youngster, but the stranger did not see them.

Abe took no chance on a sighting being made. He raised his sixgun and softly called. *"Don't you move a damned finger!"*

The man was stunned. He obeyed implicitly but probably because he had been taken so thoroughly by surprise. Then he perceptibly turned his head slightly in the direction of that harsh command, and got another command.

"You son of a bitch; one more move and I'll kill you!"

This time the man did not move even his head. He stood like a statue.

Abe waited a long time before slowly arising so that the stranger could see him. He started forward to disarm the prisoner. "Turn," he ordered. "Set your back to me, and you lousy horse-thief you, raise both hands as high as you can and stand still."

Abe disarmed the man, pushed him away using the barrel of the man's own weapon, and risked looking southward. Cal saw the signal and arose with a grunt at the youth. They both walked out of the trees.

The horse-thief heard them coming, without a doubt, but he obeyed Abe to the letter by not even trying to turn his head slightly to see who was approaching.

Cal paused, squinted at the shorter,

rounder, darker man, and made a little clucking sound. Then he jerked his head at Sandy and the two of them approached the big front entrance to that dark-looking prehistoric cave.

Abe swung his sixgun like a maul. It crushed down through the horse-thief's hat, through his hair into his skull and he dropped without a sound.

The boy's head bobbed as though he were having difficulty swallowing then he turned and would not look in the direction of the inert lump in the grass.

Cal was less concerned. As he stepped past and glanced down he said, "His gatherings are probably all cached in the cave," and preceded Abe in there leaving the lad to enter behind the older men.

The horse-thief — at least they knew he was that, and otherwise they could only speculate — had evidently been supplying his cave for a long while. On improvised, gouged-out walls in the stone and earthen cave he had created shelves and had surprisingly stocked them with a great variety of food, most of it tinned, and that made Cal and Abe look in wonder. To their knowledge there was no town, hence no store, within an awful lot of miles from this place, and if the renegade's horse had died . . . how had he accomplished all this?

"Before the horse died," said Cal, and moved to where the man's bedroll was. Beside it was a Winchester in a carbine-boot, an extra sixgun hanging by its trigger-guard upon a twig forced into the earth beside the bedroll, and a box of white candles along with a saddle, blanket and bridle, and a pair of dark-brown old U.S. Cavalry saddlebags, the kind which were large enough to hold a man's entire wardrobe, if he rode for a living.

Cal turned back towards the cave's opening, ignoring some prehistoric drawings of long-extinct bison and other animals which gifted but unknown ancient hunters had etched with great care upon the walls and ceilings of the cave. They had colouring added, mostly a rusty very dark red colour, but there was not sufficient light coming from the front of the cave to make these ancient pictures very legible even to people who might be interested in them, which Cal and Abe were not. They had seen dozens of this kind of cave-decoration in the forgotten places of the low desert and its environs; they had meant nothing to them at those other times, and this time they meant even less because of the condition under which they had encountered them. As Abe walked back towards the daylight he could understand perfectly why the unconscious man out in the grass had stolen their mounts, but that only partially mitigated what the man had done, and it in no way *excused* what he had done.

What interested Abe most of all, now that they had their horses back, and the man who had stolen them was also their prisoner, was who he was, where he was from, and what he had done — somewhere — to be so furtive and elusive.

There probably was something in his saddlebags or maybe in his pockets which would shed light, but as they walked forth from the cave they got an answer to one question which had interested them earlier when they had marvelled at the fugitive having so much in the way of shelved provisions.

Abe stepped to the cave's front opening with Cal a few steps behind and the lad up beside Cal, when from a considerable distance Abe caught a flash of reflected sunlight off metal or glass — and it was moving!

Without a second of hesitation Abe sprang backwards, nearly collided with Cal, and when his partner swore Abe pointed beyond the opening in the direction of the distant forest, lying north-easterly.

"Someone is coming. Hell's bells, I never thought there was *two* of 'em!"

Abe turned briefly to glare at the boy, but Sandy Weatherby was as surprised as Abe and would have stepped ahead to look but Cal caught his arm and held him back there in the interior gloom.

Cal said, "That's why the one in the grass was comin' from that direction, Abe. He was expectin' this other one; he was over there to look for him and maybe to welcome him; anyway, I'd guess that's why he was over yonder."

Abe looked at Sandy again, stormily. "You never mentioned there being two of 'em!"

"I never saw but this one; the stocky, dark-looking man. That's all I ever saw out here. If he had a partner, I know for a fact he hasn't been around for a long while or else I'd at least have seen his tracks."

Abe turned back slowly to watching the distant fringe of trees. There was no additional indication of movement over there for a long while, not until a mounted man drifted indifferently from the trees and rode a few yards looking hard in the direction of the cave, then turned back up through the trees again, apparently expecting to be seen and greeted, and when this had not hap-

94

pened, turning back to the shelter of the forest.

The horseman did not act fearful nor furtive, but even if he'd had occasion to feel wary he was now in a place where the chances of difficulty even if he were to meet someone seemed very slight. That was the impression the watchers in the cave got when the rider left the trees, then returned to them.

Cal said, "Gawddamn! For a ghost-town and an uninhabited countryside, this blasted territory is runnin' over with folks. Well, we can wait in here and clean that one out like we cleaned out the other one."

Abe had doubts. "I didn't hit that one in the grass that hard, Cal. He's not goin' to lie still forever."

They inched ahead to locate the man in the forest and did not see him although occasionally they could hear his progress.

The man lying in the grass was still there, in a lifeless lump, but as Abe had thought and as Cal had said, he was not going to lie like that all day.

Abe waited for the oncoming rider to show himself, and when he did not do it Abe swore annoyedly, because he did not want to go forth and drag their unconscious prisoner inside the cave until he knew he could safely do it, but he was also certain that the unconscious man would probably recover about the time his oncoming acquaintance reached the cave-area.

It was Sandy Weatherby who solved the problem. "That rider's got to go plumb around to the blind side of this rock ledge before he comes down alongside and out into the meadow where he can see the cave. If you want, I'll show you."

Cal shook his head. "You stay right where you are," he commanded, then he stepped past Abe to the cave's opening, studied the territory where he thought the rider had to be, about this time, and finally he turned back and smiled at his partner.

Abe said, "You sure?" and Cal nodded. "Plumb sure. Anyway at that distance he probably can't hit you."

Abe glared, balefully waggled his head, then stepped forth. He had all the confidence in the world in his partner's judgement, but it was standard procedure to act very sceptical.

He had no trouble at all reaching the place where the downed man was lying. Without ceremony he grabbed cloth and turned to begin dragging. The limp form moaned a little but otherwise did not make a sound and at no time made any attempt to rise or struggle. He allowed himself to be dragged.

Abe was surprised at the man's weight. He had not seemed to be as heavy as he turned out to be.

Almost to the cave's opening, he heard horseshoes among the rattling chat along the north side of the stone ledge where the stranger was moving steadily forward, He increased his effort and Cal rushed forth to callously grab an arm and also tug. They got their burden yanked into the dust of the cave's foremost area just as a horseman emerged a few hundred yards northward and instead of turning directly towards the cave, rode with obvious interest out across the grassland to where the sorrel and black were grazing.

Abe let go of the inert man, who promptly fell flat and lay there looking more dead than alive. Cal made his little clucking sound and dragged the captive by his one arm, farther back. This time, the man's groan had more feeling to it. He seemed to be coming round, finally.

Cal gestured towards the canteen near that flat-out bedroll and the youth antici-pated his order by stepping over to grab the container and return with it.

Cal removed the cap, wrinkled his nose, cocked a suspicious eye downward, sniffed again, then ignored the man in the dust and tasted the canteen's contents. It was not water it was whisky!

Cal took another swallow, then a third one, and finally sank to one knee to hoist their prisoner and with the boy's help pour whisky down their captive. That simple act accomplished more than two more hours of lying on the ground might have done, The prisoner gagged, choked and retched, then tried to thresh and pull back.

Cal put the canteen aside, lifted out his sixgun and pointed it directly at the renegade's face. "Shut up and quit makin' noise," he ordered.

The prisoner obeyed, but he turned red in the face from an effort not to cough. Apparently, for all that his canteen had whisky in it, the man was not a seasoned drinker.

But at least he was now fully conscious.

Cal put up the gun and raised his eyes to the boy. Sandy was a little diffidently eyeing the man with the lump on his head and the blood-matted hair under his hat where Abe had struck him over the head. To the boy, that particular renegade was clearly someone to fear.

8
THE FOURSOME

Cal helped their prisoner to his feet then pushed him relentlessly forward until Abe turned, looked at them both, then moved to implement what he knew Cal had in mind. They positioned the sore-headed fugitive in the cave opening, told him under no circumstances to move or make a sound, then all four of them, the boy included, watched that distant rider go out and around the pair of grazing horses making what was clearly a very interested appraisal.

The impression that horseman gave was of someone who had been quite surprised to find those two horses out there, and who was just about as much surprised to find that the horses were valuable animals.

Finally, the horseman halted, lifted his hat, vigorously scratched while glancing in the direction of the cave, then dropped the hat back down and lifted his rein-hand.

Abe prompted their prisoner. "Step ahead

where he can see you, mister, raise an arm and beckon him on in."

As the prisoner shuffled forward Cal said, "For all we know there is another one. Hell, there wasn't even supposed to be this fresh one."

Abe, who was intently watching their prisoner obey his order offered no answer and Cal turned to make certain the lad was out of the way, then swung forward to watch the horseman begin riding slowly in the direction of the cave.

That was when Abe said "If there's a third one it's going to get kind of crowded in here."

The rider came up close enough for the hiding men to see his face and riding gear quite distinctly. Abe said, "He's bringing in supplies . . . So that's how this one we caught got this place so darned well provisioned."

Out in the sunshine the stranger swung off, trailed his reins and strolled forward as casually as though he had no reason to be suspicious, and apparently he didn't have because the silent man stiffly standing in the cave entrance was all the stranger had expected to find there.

When he finally left the horse standing and walked on up, speaking to the silent onlooker in the cave-opening, he smiled and acted completely natural. He was not quite close enough yet to notice the unnatural stance of his friend.

"Figured for a minute or two you had visitors when I seen those horses out yonder, Chet. Where'n hell's your animal?"

Chet stiffly replied. "My horse upped and died."

The smiling man chuckled. "Where'd you steal them two, then?"

"Down in the village," replied the prisoner, and started to say something else but his friend was within a yard or two of the cave opening, and both the men in the darkness back yonder quietly stepped forward with guns.

The smiling man's reaction of total surprise left him as astonished as the other man had been when he too had first seen another man near the cave; he looked from Abe to his gun, then over to Cal and his gun. Finally, he saw the lad, studied him momentarily and swung his gaze back to the fugitive in the cave opening. "Thanks," he said very dryly, and Chet was distressed enough to raise his hands, palms upwards.

"What'n hell could I do?"

Cal strolled ahead. He was tall, but the stranger in front of him was just as tall, and in fact they both had that lanky, lean build of many rawboned individuals. They looked one another directly in the eye as Cal removed the newcomer's sixgun and stepped away.

Abe leaned on the cave-wall eyeing the second man. "You got a name?" he asked, and the stranger's lips curled.

"Yeah. Jack Jones."

Abe was unperturbed. "Jack, pull up your britches so's we can see if you got a boot-knife, then dump everything from your pockets into your hat."

While they all stood watching, the new-comer obeyed to the letter, and when he straightened up and glanced wryly at Abe, he said, "You're no damned lawman."

Abe neither confirmed this nor denied it, he in fact, ignored it to ask a question of "Jack Jones". "Where are you two fellers wanted?"

Chet and Jack exchanged a swift glance, then Jack answered in a seemingly forthright manner. "Eastern Canada. One hell of a long ways from here." Jack paused, then said, "Bank robbery." He studied Abe for a moment, put his head a little to one side and said, "Where are you fellers wanted?"

Abe did not answer. He was beginning to speculate beyond this moment. He and Cal were not lawmen, for a fact; neither were they bounty-hunters. In fact, all they had ever wanted since riding north up out of Mexico, was to peacefully arrive upon the north-country cattle ranges where they could get riding jobs. What they most specifically did not want, was a couple of prisoners, outlaws or not.

They had brushed with the law a long time earlier, had managed to maintain a very low and unobtrusive profile ever since, and this spring had decided to head north and test their anonymity.

So far, every blessed time they turned around, they bumped into something notorious; either a crazy man, a gun-stealing kid, a handsome widow-woman, or a pair of genuine fugitives.

Abe holstered his Colt and dryly said, "Well, it's a darned crowded territory, but I expect we might as well eat." And without offering anything more than that he gestured Jack inside the cave.

Food was no problem, nor did either of the unsmiling silent fugitives offer either Cal or Abe reason to draw their guns again as they stood back and watched those two start a meal.

They had not forgotten Sandy Weatherby, but neither had they included him up until now when he came over and quietly said, "I got to be getting home. My mother'll be worried if I don't show up directly."

They looked at him as though he were another problem — which, of course, he was. Cal stepped past, went back where Chet's bedroll and "possibles" were, detached the Winchester in its leather boot, came forward and without a word handed the weapon to the lad. "Tell her we gave it to you," he said, and smiled. Then he turned. "Abe . . . ?"

The problem presented by the youth was a nebulous one; as far as Abe was concerned they probably owed the youth their gratitude; on the other hand he had never really demonstrated compatibility. Particularly toward Abe Bannion.

Now, they were encouraging him; they had armed him and had allowed him to trail along after they had reached the meadow where their missing animals were, but basically Abe's misgivings were the result of the fact that he knew nothing about boys Sandy's age.

All he was confident of was that they had armed the lad, and now they were going to turn him loose. Abe shrugged his shoulders; if they kept him, his mother would be frantic; if they turned him loose what was to prevent him from returning by stealth?

"Yeah," murmured Abe. "Well, get along home, Sandy, and we're right obliged for your help and all. And boy, stay there! You hear?"

The boy nodded gravely in Abe's direction, then turned to fleetingly smile at Cal, ignore the captives, and rush forth from the cave on his hurrying way homeward. One of the prisoners raised his head quizzically. Abe said, "He lives hereabouts with his widowed mother. How long does it take you fellers to make a simple meal, anyway!"

"Jack Jones" reared back to pause and roll a smoke. He had become more easy, or more bold depending on one's outlook, and now as he lighted up and exhaled he studied his captors. Finally, he jutted with the cigarette towards Abe and said, "I've seen you. I can't for the life of me remember where, but I've seen you."

To Abe Bannion it was unimportant whether they had ever met before. Without much doubt they had both visited a lot of cow-country communities, and because in all the range-country between the Missouri River and the Pacific Ocean there were not a vast number of towns, men who moved around a lot probably saw one another from time to time.

In fact, it was common for men to meet in cow camps — or outlaw caves — and remember having seen one another elsewhere without being even acquainted. Abe had had this happen before, especially over the line in Mexico.

Men who had reason to "winter" beyond the reach of federal and territorial law in Chihuahua or Sonora were, in fact, never so numerous that they did not recall seeing one another down there. On this basis Abe said, "You spent much time in Mexico?" and when "Jack Jones" smiled without committing himself, Abe said, "That's probably where it was . . . But that's even farther from eastern Canada."

"We didn't start out from there," explained Jack. "That just happened to be where we went to rob a big bank because it was so far off. Originally, we came from Texas . . . You?"

Abe considered "Jack Jones's" genial countenance. It was Chet who never seemed willing to smile and who looked constantly fearful. "Most anywhere," Abe said. "We been in Texas a time or two. And a lot of other places."

"Mexico?"

"Yeah, all last winter." Abe's gaze narrowed. "You're a nosey cuss, mister."

"Jack Jones" responded almost indifferently to that accusation. "Mister, I don't figure you're going to haul us down to some city, and I don't figure you're going to hang around keepin' us prisoner forever, neither. The way I got this figured, you're up in here because you don't much want a whole lot of company neither. You and your partner. Well, that puts the four of us in the same canoe, don't it?" "Jack Jones" smiled. He looked boyish when he did that although Abe and Cal had already decided he was at least as old as they were.

"Gents," he went on, in his folksy, friendly way, "I figure we're pretty much the same; been tarred from the same brush. I don't know what you fellers done and I don't especially want to know, but I'll bet you a pawful of gold money you're also wanted somewhere . . . Well, that pretty much leaves us right about where we are right this minute without there bein' much future in this companionship. How do you see it, mister?"

"Like you should have been a minister," growled Abe, and sniffed as Chet began dishing hash into tin plates.

Cal strolled ahead to accept the plate held out to him. He and "Jack Jones" exchanged a direct look. Jack smiled and Cal's expression remained stonily impassive.

The food was passable. In spite of the variation to be found upon the provision-shelves, Chet and his partner had cooked bully-beef with flour gravy; it tasted exactly like every blessed meat-meal rangemen got at every blessed cow-camp from one end of the West to the other end, but it was filling.

Someone had once observed that so was sawdust and it tasted the same.

The coffee was welcome though. To men accustomed to very strong, bitter-tasting coffee, what Cal and Abe got in the cave was one degree better because it had not been boiled quite as long as coffee usually was boiled.

"Jack Jones" looked up from where he was sitting cross-legged and said, "I ran across some shod-horse tracks going north from the ghost-town. I followed them because they were fresh, and that's why I missed finding trace of you fellers, I guess. You see that other feller?"

"Loca cabeza," replied Cal, and tapped his temple, "Yeah, we met him. His name was Sampson Mortimer, and he thought it was funny folks called him Mort."

"Jack Jones" looked steadily at Cal. "What's funny about that?"

"In Mex it means death," replied Cal, and

shot a look at his partner because clearly, if "Jack Jones" didn't understand border-Spanish he hadn't been a very long while on the low desert, or below it over the line in Mexico. Not that this meant a whole lot except that every little tidbit a person learned about another person in this fugitive-country, helped a person arrive at private judgements.

Chet finally opened up. He told his partner what he had observed of Sampson Mortimer. He even admitted that it had been in the back of his mind to steal Mort's horse after his own animal died, but before he could get the scheme far enough long to implement it, Abe and Cal had also arrived in Paso Fino, and they were not only riding better animals, but they had two of them, and Chet decided to steal their horses in order to have one to ride and one to pack all his stores upon when he pulled out.

Cal stopped eating and eyed Chet all through the horse-thief's candid confession, then he sighed and went back to eating. A couple of hours earlier that kind of an admission would have got Chet hanged. Now, while it was still sufficient grounds for a lynching, the four of them had been sitting there in the cave's cool, pleasant entrance eating and exchanging views and comments so long that Cal's feelings of fierce anger had been considerably diluted.

He did, however, manage to growl a little. "If we'd caught you in the act you wouldn't be sitting over there now."

Chet looked down at the plate in his lap and went back to eating. His partner was silent, too, for a while, then he smiled at Cal and made a frank comment.

"This is a hell of a long distance from anywhere, *amigo.* Bein' afoot up here's about the same as being a snowball in hell . . . A man'd steal another feller's horse here, where he wouldn't lay a hand on someone else's critter anywhere else."

"Preacher," muttered Abe. "And that don't make it right, Jones, because if Chet here got a-horseback to ride off — where would that leave Cal and me? Afoot, that's where, and like you said, this here is a lousy place for that to happen to a feller."

"Jack Jones" smiled and made a little gesture of resignation with his hands. "All right, I'm not going to argue with you gents. You got the guns." He kept smiling and eating and shrewdly eyeing the armed men opposite him. Then he switched the topic. "Where was that other feller riding to?"

Neither Cal nor Abe answered because they did not remember whether Sampson

Mortimer had told them his destination. All they really remembered was that Mortimer was an exceptional cook — and was unbalanced.

The silence did not trouble "Jack Jones". He was evidently one of those irrepressible individuals who accepted rebuffs as though they meant nothing. Maybe, some of the time they didn't mean anything. Maybe, in fact, that wasn't a bad way to be.

For Abe Bannion the easy new association between the four of them presaged his and Cal Madison's withdrawal — with their horses — as soon as possible.

As for the horse-thief, Abe was as relentless in his disapproval as ever, but because he had never been a hypocrite and because neither he nor his partner were models of virtue, as he finished eating he began to simply wish he and Cal were out of this and on their way, and it was also in the back of his mind that if they ever came north over the line again, and took that damned old-time road again, under no circumstances would he consent to take the westerly fork again!

9
TO THE RESCUE

The boy returned riding an old bay horse with white around his muzzle and his eyes. Even when they heard the rider coming the sound was not that of a vigorous young horse, and when they went outside, all four of them, and watched the lad break clear of the trees, because each of them knew horse flesh they did not have to comment, but that bay animal had seen his best day probably a few years before his rider had been born.

The boy urged his mount into a trot as he came out into the grassland and saw those four men over there watching. The horse responded without either enthusiasm or life, but he obeyed, he began to make an ungainly trot in the direction of the cave. The boy, who was riding bareback, sat upon that distinctly uncomfortable back-bone with forbearance. He had his Winchester balanced upon his upper leg, pointing skyward, the way bronco Indians rode.

Jones said, "Don Quixote," and got a chary look from the other three men as he smiled at the approaching youth and shook his head.

Abe did not smile; he had ordered the boy to stay home and here it was less than an hour and a half with the boy back again. "Ought to kick his rear," he growled, and Cal agreed with reservations.

"All right, but first let's find out what brings him back."

The wait was short. When Sandy got close he leaned and looked over his shoulder in an unmistakable way. Men like those out front of the cave who had spent their share of time looking back over shoulders had no difficulty in interpreting the boy's gesture.

Chet said, "Hell! He's bein' followed. He's leadin' someone right on up here!"

The boy covered the final distance through thick meadow grass and hauled down to a halt, with the ancient bay readily anticipating the pull on his reins. As Sandy slid to the ground and started forward he said, "When I got home there was three rangemen there . . . . They was tryin' to make my mother come out, and they'd already ransacked the barn and had what harness we had left on their horses . . . I shot one of them!"

The men gazed almost dispassionately at the agitated youth.

"The other two came after me . . . I ran into the forest before they could get clear of the yard, and I found our old buggy horse and . . ."

"And you brought them up here," exclaimed Chet angrily, then stepped over where he'd have a clear view. "How far back are they?"

The question required no answer. A pair of cowboys came out of the yonder trees at a stiff-legged trot. They saw the distant bay horse and increased their gait, but evidently they did not notice the four men standing on the far side of the bay horse with the boy until they had loped a couple of dozen yards. Then they saw them.

Abe shouldered past the youth with a growled curse. Cal gestured for Chet and Jones to do the same, then Cal came up behind all the others.

The rangeriders stopped dead-still and sat like stone, studying as much as they could make out of the small group in front of the cave. Neither of those rangeriders had a booted carbine but they both wore shell-belts and sixguns.

Abe reached for Sandy's carbine, levered up a load and took four steps ahead, dropped to one knee and aimed. Those two rangemen whirled and sank in spurs. They fled at break-neck speed back to the protection of the trees. Nor did they slacken pace when they got down there, but at considerable risk went charging on through and out of sight.

For a few moments it was possible to hear those men, then the silence resettled and as Abe turned, Jones was shaking his head in the direction of Sandy Weatherby. That annoyed Abe, so he growled.

"Well, what would you have done — sprouted wings and flown away?"

The fugitive said, "They'll be back, whoever they are, and they'll fetch along someone's whole blessed riding crew."

"Who says we got to still be here?" asked Abe, handing back the carbine.

As Sandy accepted his Winchester Chet eyed the gun with a rueful expression, but he said nothing. Even if he meant to he would not have had the opportunity because Cal had an observation to make.

"Somebody's going to ride-double away from here, or he's going to walk."

Cal was looking narrowly at Chet, the only one among them who did not have a horse.

Sandy broke in speaking shakily. "They'll go back and fire our house. They were threatening to do that when they were yelling at my mother; they were saying if she didn't come out they'd burn the house with her in it . . . They'll do it, too. Those are Cactus riders."

"They are what?" demanded Jones.

"Cactus," restated the lad. "That's the colonel's branch; a big cactus-lookin' mark on the ribs of his cattle and on the left shoulder of his horses. Those were his riders. I've seen them before skulkin' around our place tryin' to catch my maw outside. I've seen them . . ." Sandy turned an appealing look to Cal. "Please help us. Don't let them burn the house."

It was the horse-thief Chet who said, "Will that old rack of bones pack double, boy?"

Before Sandy could answer Cal nudged Abe. "Come along; what the hell difference will it make if we get into a damned silly war with a bunch of rangemen; we already got involved in a whole bunch of other silly darned foolishness."

Abe turned to Jones. "Take Chet up behind you. The lad's old horse isn't up to it."

Jones nodded. "Sure, and after me and Chet get over there what are we supposed to do — throw rocks?"

Abe gestured. "Go in there and get your

darned guns, and by gawd if you get cute . . . ! Hurry up, we don't have forever!"

Abe and Cal went out to catch their horses and fashion squaw-bridles of rope. Fortunately, both animals had been well-cared for and had round backs. Both the men grunted up to ride bareback. When the four of them were ready to ride, with Jones carrying his partner behind the cantle. Chet called to Sandy and held out his hand for the Winchester.

The lad looked uncertainly at Cal, who growled at Chet. "You lucky bastard, that's the price of us not hangin' you for a lousy horse-thief! It's the lad's gun from now on!"

They left the area of the cave at a fast walk which eventually broke over into an easy lope. The lad fell steadily to the rear because his old horse could not keep up. Cal thought it was just as well. So did Abe.

Chet and "Jack Jones" did not appear to notice. Once, when their over-burdened mount dropped down to a long-legged kidney-punching trot, Chet cried out profanely. Jones promptly gigged the horse over into that easy lope again. Otherwise, those two seemed perfectly agreeable to what they were about to become involved with. The difference which had formerly existed between captives and captors atrophied too, until the four of them were calling back and forth as Abe led the way. He and Cal had been over through this south-westerly broken country before. They could answer the basic questions of route and distance, but when Jones asked about the Cactus Cow outfit, neither Abe nor Cal could make a single enlightening comment; they had never before heard of such a ranch either.

The ride back down out of the mountains was swiftly made; it was nearly all downhill. Once they reached the open country Abe slackened to a steady, slogging walk, and it was because of this lessening of their haste no doubt which allowed Sandy to eventually catch up.

He did not quite overtake them but he was within hailing distance south of the final rank of trees when he called in a high voice and made several elaborate gestures due westward.

The men halted and sat a moment looking back. "He knows this country a darned sight better'n we do," Cal said, "and the fact is, riding straight down there in plain sight like a flock of pigeons don't set too well with me. Those bastards'll be figurin' on us coming like that."

They turned westward and gestured for the boy to meet them. That way no one actually retraced his tracks nor lost any time, and by the time they were a mile westward with a fine dark background of trees to shield them from all but very close scrutiny, the lad was over there on his old horse.

"They'll see you before you can get close," Sandy told them. "There's a way from up here that a feller can come down to the yard and keep the barn between him and the main-yard over by the house. I'll show you."

The bay horse collected himself for a gallop and no doubt because he knew exactly where he was heading — for home and maybe a tin of grain and a bait of hay, he did not begin to shuffle and fall away until they had the buildings in sight. By then the four men no longer needed a guide.

Cal leaned to touch the lad's leg as he prepared to speed ahead, and said, "You stay back here. Winchester or no Winchester, you do what I say!"

Cal allowed Sandy no chance to argue, nor even to agree; he gigged his black gelding and went out after the others in a long-legged lope.

They covered all the intervening distance without difficulty, but when they got near the buildings Jones signalled for a halt. He had been gauging distances and now he said, "We're darned near in carbine range, gents."

Abe made a short answer. "Those two didn't have carbines, only belt-guns."

Jones grinned. "You know, if a man is wrong just once in this kind of a fix he sure-Lord isn't likely to ever be wrong again . . . All right, mister, you ride on another hundred yards."

Abe was disgusted so he turned and reined out, keeping the barn in front as he progressed that additional hundred yards and when he halted to watch ahead, looking for any kind of movement at all, the pair of outlaws riding double, booted out their animal as Cal loped easily past.

Nothing happened. They got all the way to the rear of the barn and had dismounted before they even heard anything, and all that noise amounted to was Sandy coming in his shambling trot.

Cal handed Abe the reins to his black and as Abe joined Chet and Jones in leading their animals inside to be stalled, Cal went back angrily to berate the youth. But when Sandy got up there he slackened to a walk, still holding that Winchester upon his upper leg like an old-time bronco, and before Cal could snarl Sandy said, "Mister, it's my mother. My paw wouldn't have wanted *me*

120

to hang back and *he* wouldn't have done it neither."

Cal puffed out his cheek, then said something harsh under his breath and gestured for the lanky youth to climb off and lead his horse into the barn as the others had done.

There was no sign of two ridden-down Cactus outfit horses nor the men who had been riding them. But they did find some soggy, bloodstained rags in the barn, and they also found where a man had been lying until a pair of men wearing run-over old boots had hoisted him up astraddle a horse. The horse-tracks went off north-westerly.

Jones asked Sandy where the Cactus Cattle Company was, and the lad lifted a thin arm to point. The men looked at one another; that wounded rangerider had ridden off in the direction Sandy had indicated.

The reason those two surviving rangemen had not been able to overtake the boy on his old nag was clearly spelled out in those barn-tracks where they had waited to help their wounded companion; to make a bandage for him, to get him up atop his horse, and to head him in the correct direction before going after their own horses to take up the pursuit, by which time the terrified youngster had got as much of a head-start as he could get on that ancient fine-harness horse.

They went through to the front of the barn, gingerly peeked and killed time and speculated. There was no sign of the pair of Cactus cowboys.

Abe called Sandy on up, pointed to the main-house and told him to sing out. The boy obeyed and in the very next moment the front door flew open inward and the handsome black-haired, dark-eyed woman stepped forth with a too-big shellbelt around her middle and with a carbine in both her hands.

Abe sighed with relief. "Ask her where them cowboys are?" he said to the boy, and as soon as Sandy had called out the question, his mother answered that they had been gone for more than an hour.

"Didn't come back here after all," stated Cal, and stepped forth to also look up in the direction of the main-house. Cal was just as relieved as his partner was. Cal could fight just as swiftly as anyone else would but if there was a way to decently avoid having to fight he was also very willing to do that.

The woman at the main-house called towards the barn "Son, who is with you?"

'Those two men who came out last night

from Paso Fino."

"Ask them to come to the house, Sandy."

Cal did not wait to be invited. He did not even look over his shoulder at his partner, he simply stepped forth and started walking. Abe watched a moment, then did the same. The last to leave the barn were Chet and Jones, and they came along only when Abe turned and jerked his head at them.

10
ABE'S IDEA

Abe handled the introductions and he did it without an inkling that he and his partner were not old friends of the pair of bank-robbers, and the fact that Sandy had not spoken to his mother since participating in the capture of the bank-robbers prevented her from knowing any more about the newcomers than Abe chose to tell her, which was practically nothing at all.

Clearly, the fugitives were not only surprised at finding an inhabited ranch out here but were equally as astonished to discover such a handsome woman living there. When she offered them coffee both Jones and Chet instantly accepted. They did it in the manner of men seeking to prolong an interlude in their lives which was very pleasant to them both.

Sandy's mother smiled, which was something she had not done the night Abe and Cal had got undetected inside the house.

She confirmed what her son had said, but she'd had no idea who had shot that rangerider until the men told her, then she seemed divided between engulfing her son with weary gratitude, and staring in disapproval at him. Abe got them through that moment by asking about the rangemen.

She confirmed who they were, but instead of simply saying they were Cactus Ranch riders and that their employer was the "colonel" as her son had said, she named the owner as Colonel Tim Canfield and explained that Cactus cowboys harassed her constantly; she thought, too, they were responsible for her livestock disappearing, but there was no way to prove it. She said that she rarely rode forth any more, now that the cattle and horses were gone, all but a few head, and when she did ride out she carried her ivory-stocked derringer, her dead husband's sixgun, and either a carbine or a rifle.

The men sat in the kitchen while she got them coffee and set forth some oatmeal cookies she had made. They were nearly as hard as rock-candy but to men who had not even come within fragrance-distance of woman-baking of any kind in many moons, those cookies along with that fresh coffee were an adequate reward for the long ride from up by the cave.

Sandy went out back and returned from the well-house with a jar of preserves. His mother set out fresh-baked bread, but there was no butter since the milk cow had vanished.

The men ate, and listened, and smiled a lot, even Chet, who ordinarily did not seem to like to smile very much, and by the time they had finished the coffee, all the cookies and most of the baked bread, they had heard much more than the handsome woman had told Abe and Cal.

None of it was exactly a new story, but then as Abe said when the men adjourned to the front porch to smoke, none of the bad things which happened in this life ever seemed to be happening for the first time. He looked at Chet and "Jack Jones", the two unknown quotients, as he voiced his thoughts.

"We're due up north directly, me and my partner. It seems sort of a shame though to pass through here and not at least get these folks back their milk cow."

"If it's still around," said Chet.

"If it ain't," stated Jones, "why then maybe we could get them another one."

"And their horses," put in Cal. "Hell of a note, being almost afoot this far out . . .

And they once had a little band of cattle, gents. How are folks supposed to make flour and bean money unless they got a few big yearlings to trail down to some town and peddle?"

Chet rubbed his bristly jaw. "Where is this Cactus Ranch, and just how many riders has this colonel got?"

Those two things were certainly the most important questions requiring answers. It was one thing to be gallant and it was something altogether different to ride to death against big and deadly odds; that way a man didn't help a darned soul; instead he hindered them.

Cal went back into the house to hunt up Sandy and get the information the men needed. During his absence Abe eyed the pair of fugitives from a doubting set of narrowed eyes.

He appreciated the attitude of the pair of strangers; it was his private opinion that any kind of men would have felt the militant antagonism towards Colonel Canfield and his cow ranch which he and his partner felt. On the other hand, he knew very little about the bank-robbers; that is, he knew nothing at all about them when it came to having them stand beside him, and Cal, in a serious confrontation. If they were a pair of those summertime heroes who melted at the first sight of guns in the hands of enemies, why then Abe and Cal were probably going to get buried hereabouts, because no matter how many or how few riders Colonel Canfield had, it was bound to be a hell of a lot more than two!

He was right. Cal returned to the war-council on the porch. "Cactus is four miles north-west," he reported, "and that gen'l or whatever he is as owns the place keeps six riders . . . Missus Weatherby told me her husband used to say Cactus never hired nothin' but border-jumpers. Damned tough men."

For a while there was no further discussion. Jones went to work rolling a cigarette and his partner stood on the porch gazing out over the vast emptiness towards the mountains. Finally he said, "We dassn't," to the man calling himself Jones, and Cal slid a knowing look at Abe, then Cal said, "Canada's a hell of a distance from the uplands above the low desert, Chet. If I was in your boots I wouldn't be hiding in no darned cave for something I did a thousand miles from here."

Chet and Jones exchanged a look, then the talkative, genial outlaw exhaled smoke and spoke out. "Well, we robbed that bank right enough, gents. What my partner's workin' up a sweat over is that we also stopped a coach over near Las Crucas a month or so back, and a couple of months before that we raided a bank in the Panhandle."

Cal looked sardonic. He had expected nothing less than this kind of an admission. It had never made much sense for men to be hiding in the low desert country near the Mexican border when all they'd done was raid a bank up in Canada somewhere.

Abe didn't view the peril as being very critical. "No one's going to be up here snooping around from over in the Texas Panhandle or from Las Crucas. Hell, we're miles from either of those places . . . Well, but it'll be up to you gents. Cal and I'll hang around and see if maybe we can't at least get back the lady's milk cow . . . That's a pretty darned lousy way to act when a woman's widowed and all . . ."

Jones said, "What the hell, Chet; a couple of days of teaching some lousy cow outfit how to act towards folks . . . ?"

Chet did not turn from where he was standing looking towards the mountains although he did shift the position of his head a little, and finally when he spoke, he also raised a rigid arm.

"Damned decision has already been made gents!"

The dust was distant in the mellow sunlight but it was not being made by wind or by cattle or by free-running livestock at all because it was holding to a very direct south-easterly course.

"Cactus," said Chet. "Sure as hell. Those two who didn't come down here to burn the lady out run for home and now they're comin' back with the whole crew."

"Minus one," murmured his partner, "Jack Jones", who also stepped to the front railing and stood hands in pockets gazing far out. "Gents, by gawd we just stood around here jawing like a bunch of greenhorns and here they come. Primed and loaded for bear sure as I'm a foot tall." He turned, smiling.

The Widow Weatherby had also seen those riders approaching across the distant sun-washed grassland and came to the doorway to rigidly stand with her husband's Winchester in the crook of one arm.

"You should have ridden away," she murmured, white in the face.

Abe and Jones looked at one another. Jones smiled at the handsome woman. He had more of a knack with words. "Ma'm, bread and cookies like that . . . How many will there be, do you reckon?"

"With Colonel Canfield, there could be seven men, but if one was hurt . . ."

"Yeah," stated Jones. "Six. Four of us; that adds up to fair odds."

The woman's dark eyes drifted from face to face. "Five to six," she said, correcting Jones. From behind her in the doorway her son's changing voice said, "Six to six," and the men turned and smiled. Even Chet and Abe smiled, and in the very moment while everyone was silently standing watching the forward progress of those riders, steeped in their private thoughts, Abe put forth a suggestion.

"Cal, suppose you and Chet stay here at the house with the Weatherbys. Jack and I'll see if we can scat out the south way and get around those fellers and head back for their home place." He turned to face his partner. "If we make it, watch the sky, we'll fire an outbuilding."

Chet scowled. "They are goin' to see you leave."

Abe conceded that. "Yeah; riding southward like we're running away. I don't expect they'll chase us; anyway that'll sort of be up to you lads. If you can stall 'em one way or another until we can swing around and ride north-west . . ." He looked at the handsome dark-eyed woman. "Due north-west a few miles, ma'm?"

She nodded. "You'll see it. You can't help but see it."

Abe looked at the boy in the doorway behind his mother. Then he winked at his partner as he said, "You'll have a pretty respectable little army. See you maybe tonight some time. Come along, Jack."

No one spoke as the two of them went down off the porch and across the yard in the direction of the barn. Even the bank-robber was silent until they were inside the barn and he stepped out back to assess the distance still separating the oncoming rangemen from the ranch-yard. As he returned and Abe told him to hurry up and get rigged out, the outlaw said, "You figure splitting me and Chet will fix it so's you and your partner can still keep an eye on us?"

Abe was leading his horse out of the barn when he answered. "Something wrong with doing that? What do I know about either of you — in a pinch?"

Jack was handy at saddling and bridling. He led his animal forth, toed in and rose up across leather, and smiled at Abe. "All right; I don't blame you for lookin' a little out," he said, and reined around.

They left the yard by passing alongside the main-house to the east, over across the open area where Abe and Cal had tried to cross on their first, nocturnal, visit to the Weatherby ranch. The people on the porch waved. Abe and Jack waved back then lifted their horses into a slogging trot; an uncomfortable gait unless a man stood in the stirrups, Moorish style.

Cactus Ranch was still back there, and now it seemed that they might have detected the departure of a pair of riders from the ranch because they picked up their pace somewhat, came steadily onward in a lunging gallop. But if they'd possessed wings they still would not have been able to get close to those two south-bound horsemen.

Eventually, it seemed that they did not have in mind making a chase out of it, probably because they had already been pushing their saddle-animals, and the horses were not able to suddenly break out in a miles-long race with men riding fresher horses.

Abe stood in the stirrups gazing back. The man at his side scoffed. "They couldn't catch us if they tried, and it don't look to me like they'll try."

Abe eased down in the saddle, booted his horse over into an easy lope and began a big long-swooping bend around from southward to westward, and eventually a mile or more out yonder, on around until they were heading north-westerly and steadily up-country.

By the time they were riding directly for the Cactus cow ranch there was no longer any sighting of those other riders. They had clearly reached the ranchyard by this time. Even their dust had settled.

Abe hauled down to a steady walk with Jack beside him rolling a cigarette and looking pleased. Perhaps because Jones seemed to be such an out-going, forthright individual he was easy to be around. Abe, who had known him something like three and a half hours, no longer than that, was at ease in Jones's company — but he still kept a watchful eye on the bank-robber.

When they had covered what Jones estimated to be a mile and a half in the proper direction, Abe said, "I don't figure it'll be like eatin' apple pie."

Jack agreed with this while studying the countryside they were crossing. "I reckon not; there'll be a *cosinero* at the place, and maybe a chore-boy and who knows who else?" Jones turned, trickling smoke and smiling. "But we can do it. For one thing they aren't goin' to suspect anything, up here."

Abe looked sceptical. "It's damned open country. Whoever's up there, if they got eyes at all, will see two riders a long while before we can get close."

Jack remained optimistic. "We'll face that when we come to it," he said, and punched out the cigarette atop his saddlehorn. Then he shot Abe a quick look with a twinkle and said, "Sure would be nice if it was dark, wouldn't it?"

Abe nodded, detected the faint-distant outline of low, dark blocks off on their left a fair distance, and pointed.

The buildings were of logs like most other cow-outfit structures in this part of the territory, and although they seemed to be darkly weathered they could not be very old for the elemental reason that until fairly recently there had been no cow outfits operating in this country from permanent headquarters.

"Like a lousy fort," said Abe.

He was correct, and that should not have surprised him; in this kind of country where a man could still kick out a cut-back or two, if he really went bronco-hunting, without a lot of effort, no one built up an isolated cow outfit, or even a town or village, without defence dictating both the setting and the architecture.

Without smiling this time, Jack said, "We sure need some darkness."

Abe silently agreed, but since they were not going to get any darkness he thought in terms of a daylight approach and decided the best way was to ride right on in the way they were heading. He said, "We got just one advantage. Whoever is left up at the ranch don't know you and me from a stray steer. I don't know what that'll be worth, but I don't figure they are going to start shooting before we do, and that ought to give us a nickel's worth of leverage."

Abe was right; when they were close enough to the yard to see someone standing across in front of the big log horse-barn with a rifle leaning at his side, it became clear that whoever the defender was, he did not have in mind opening up on them. He seemed to be standing warily rather than slouched and simply curious, but as long as he did not pick up that long-barrelled gun Abe's worry did not heighten.

They were just beyond the yard, on the fringes and facing towards the main-house when that paunchy individual in front of the horse-barn finally reached and almost lazily lifted the rifle to rest it lightly in the crook of his left arm, with his right hand ready in an instant to swing it downward and forward.

Abe sighed and plaintively said, "It must be you, Jones; he don't much like the looks of us."

Jack laughed. The sound rang musically down across the hushed ranch-yard and the man leaning on the tie-rack in front of the barn scowled slightly in bafflement. It seemed that whoever those oncoming strangers were, they were not bent on trouble. A man didn't ride up onto you with trouble in mind, and laugh.

Didn't seem likely he'd do that, anyway.

11
DISTRACTION!

Abe and his companion drew rein near the paunchy man with the rifle. Abe forced a smile and his companion, who never seemed to have to force one, also smiled. The man at the tie-rack eyed them both, then said, "You fellers riding on through or lookin' for work?"

Abe relaxed a little more as he answered with a bald-faced lie. "Lookin' for work, *amigo,* and sort of hopin' we could rest up around here for the balance of the day. Our horses been on green grass and nothing better for weeks." He considered the paunchy man; his face was pale and sweaty, his body was soft from coddling and although he probably was no older than Abe, he looked at least fifteen years older. He was a ranch-cook or Abe had never seen one. But Abe innocently said, "You the rangeboss by any chance?"

The man slowly shook his head. "I'm the

cosinero. The rangeboss is over yonder in the bunkhouse in bed. He had an accident while he was cleaning his gun; nothing serious but it'll keep him flat down for a week or so. Anyway, the colonel ain't here and until the rangeboss is back on his feet the colonel'll do the hirin' and firin'."

Abe glanced in the direction of the squatty, ugly log bunkhouse with its little plank-porch and its two small front-wall windows, then returned his attention to the cook. *"Cosinero,"* he said, "we'd sure pay for a decent meal."

The cook adamantly shook his head. "Don't no one eat between meals on the Cactus Ranch. Not a livin' darned soul! . . . But if you're still around come suppertime, you'll get fed. That's the colonel's orders." The paunchy man continued to eye this pair of mounted men. "But if you're saddle-bums, you'd better not still be here when the colonel and the crew gets back."

Abe said, "Where did they go, *amigo?* We didn't see no town except for that abandoned Mex village out yonder."

"They didn't go to town," stated the paunchy man. "They went to teach the neighbours some manners. Colonel's not a feller to make light of. Folks cross him up and they sure learn some hard lessons."

Abe said, "Sounds reasonable; sounds like the way it had ought to be out in a place like this where there's no law."

The cook snorted. "Partner, there's law all right. The colonel's law! He lays it down and he darned well enforces it."

Abe still acted as though all this met with his exact approval when he said, "Things got to be like that." Then he said, "You got a chore-boy?" and when the cook shook his head Abe also said, "You maybe got some folks up at the main-house; the colonel's missus and all?"

The cook smiled without a shred of humour. "You don't know Tim Canfield, friend. He's got no use for womenfolk. He's been a soldier most of his life and he runs this cow outfit like it was his regiment. No woman, no families, not even no real young riders on the place."

Abe accepted this and leaned to dismount as he said, "Just you and the rangeboss?" As he reached the ground and stepped to the head of his horse, reins dangling from his left hand, he made another false smile at the *cosinero*. "You don't mind if we get down and rest a little, do you?"

Abe was already off his horse and the man with him was swinging off also. It was customary to await an invitation to alight, but there were few places where this was a hard and fast rule. The cook shrugged. "Get down and stretch, if you're a mind to," he told them, and looked sidewards in the direction of the bunkhouse. "Yeah, just me and the rangeboss, and I got to get back to work so if you fellers want to kill a little time you can go over and visit with the rangeboss."

Abe nodded, half turned, then turned back. The *cosinero*'s breath came short in a gasp. He was looking at a gun in the steady hand of Abraham Bannion.

Jack walked up, relieved the cook of the long-barrelled rifle, and without a word turned still carrying the rifle to go walking across to the bunkhouse.

Abe waited in stony silence but the man in front of him whose sweat-greasy pale face was averted while he watched "Jack Jones" disappear past the bunkhouse door, finally turned and said, "Gawddamn!" in monumental disgust. He did not look at the gun again; evidently the cook's disgust was with himself. He was so chagrined he did not seem at all afraid.

Abe spoke quietly. "Not your fault."

As though they were engaging in an academic discussion the *cosinero* answered curtly. "Yes, it's my fault, mister. The last

141

thing the colonel said as them fellers rode out of the yard was for me to throw down on anyone and take 'em prisoner . . . Hell, I warn't no soldier!"

Abe jerked his head. "Walk in front of me to the bunkhouse."

The cook paused a moment to ask a question. "What you got in mind?"

"A fire," said Abe frankly, and saw the cook's pale face go even paler.

"Chris'zake," the paunchy man gasped. "Listen to me, mister; you'll stir up a hornet's nest. You don't know old Canfield."

"Walk," ordered Abe, and gestured with the gun-barrel.

The cook walked. They crossed to the bunkhouse and entered. "Jack Jones" was standing loosely at the foot of a wall-bunk talking to a heavy-set, swarthy man who hadn't shaved within the last day or so and looked more square-jawed and villainous as a result of this than he probably looked ordinarily. When Abe walked in herding the profusely perspiring cook ahead of him the man in the bunk looked, then groaned audibly and looked past at Abe.

"Who the hell are you?" he growled. Abe did not answer, he shot Jack a look and the bank-robber must have read Abe's mind; he told the paunchy man to get over beside the bed and to stand there quietly. Then Jack nodded at Abe. "Got matches?" he asked.

Abe went out onto the bunkhouse porch. Behind him he heard the wounded man in the wall-bunk profanely threaten anyone who set a fire on Cactus Ranch. He also heard "Jack Jones" cock his Colt, and after that there was not another word spoken.

Among the outbuildings there was a buggy-shed with two wagons and a top-rig in it, but Abe's conscience pricked him; not about burning the shed, but about burning the shed with those vehicles in it.

There was also a shoeing-shed, three-sided, with a sloping roof, and across from it near the horse-barn there was a thick-walled smoke-house.

There were also several additional out-buildings. Abe did not want to fire one which as it burned might ignite another building. A man who had spent his mature life being conscious of fire as an enemy, had difficulty becoming an arsonist. On the other hand by now Colonel Canfield and his border-jumpers were in the yard of the Weatherby place and nothing would distract them as much as seeing black smoke rising above their homeplace.

He went over to the shoeing-shed, felt guilty as he gazed at the row of tools hanging along the south wall, at the laboriously-constructed big bellows which fed wind into the forge, and stepped over where oak-knots and burls had been neatly stacked, as dry and rock-hard as stone.

The shed only had three sides, the front of it was wide open to every draught which the fire would suck inward. He made kindling, put coal-dust around it, dropped on a match and within seconds there was a thin, orange tongue of flame reaching upwards.

He went outside, looked in all directions before crossing back to the bunkhouse, and when the silence and emptiness assured him he was safe, he went back and stepped into the bunkhouse doorway.

Jones had not moved and neither had the pair of men he had been guarding. The cook was perspiring more profusely than ever, clearly very agitated, but the wounded, swarthy man in the wall-bunk simply lay there, propped up and savagely glaring. Whatever the outcome of all this might be, that wounded rangeboss was not going to ever forget any of it, especially this part when he'd had to lie like a baby and allow renegades to fire an out-building.

When the man's murderous dark glare reached out to Abe, the incendiarist said, "Mister, you can count your lousy blessings. The main-house won't catch, and neither will this building — with you in it . . . Jack?"

The bank-robber leathered his Colt and moved off in the direction of the door. The last thing he did was turn and beckon to the ranch-cook. He smiled wolfishly at the bed-ridden man, and herded the cook along with them on their way over to the horses.

There was a thin wisp of sooty smoke beginning to rise. Not a breath of air, not a cloud nor a sprinkling of dust was out there to impede the rising black smoke. It would be visible for a hundred miles and more.

At the rack where their horses drowsily stood in late-day sunshine, totally unconcerned, Abe ran a thumb under the cinch, snugged up the latigo and as he did this stared across the saddle-seat.

The cook was mopping his face and neck and craning around at the increasing, steady flame at the shoeing-shed. Abe said, "*Cosinero*, you tell Canfield when he gets back the next time it'll be the horse-barn, and after that the house." Abe swung his horse and mounted. "He's got some Weatherby cattle and horses — and a milk cow too, I think. If they're back on Weatherby land by tomorrow afternoon, fine. If not, he can fort up and detail his riders all around here and we'll still burn him out down to his bootheels. You tell the old son of a bitch that, hear?"

The cook nodded and mopped sweat and silently watched the pair of horsemen jog eastward over behind the burning shed and farther, going steadily out of gun-range before they slackened gait a little and looked back.

The black smoke was rising in voluminous billows. It went straight up and Abe's former estimate, that it would be visible for a hundred miles, was two hundred miles shy of just how far it really would be visible.

"Jack Jones" rode comfortably slouched in the saddle. Now and then he would look back but most of the time he was watching the southward open country. When he came down the far side of a long-spending land-swell, and there was no way for him to be seen, he said, "If that colonel's got any sense he won't go chargin' straight back there — he'll fan his riders out like videttes."

Abe nodded. "You were in the army?"

"Three years," replied "Jack Jones", and smiled. "Captain, by gawd. Captain of the Second Georgia Sharpshooters."

"Secesh," murmured Abe, without particular rancour.

Jones nodded. "Yeah, Confederate. You?"

"Union. Fourth Missouri Cavalry." Abe smiled back. "The First, Second and Third went to the South. Fourth, Fifth and Sixth went to the Union."

Jones continued to gaze over at Abe, and finally he said, "Captain Grover Reasoner."

Abe nodded. "Private Abraham Bannion." He grinned again, and as they picked up the gait a little in order to have a lot of territory around them in case they needed it, they both laughed. When they hauled down to a fast walk another mile onward the bank-robber named Grover Reasoner waved with an upraised arm. "If Canfield's got a lick of sense he'll figure whoever raided the ranch will head either east, west, or straight north into the mountains." He dropped the arm and shot Abe a look. "As ranking person here, I'll give my opinion first. He'll fan 'em out on a skirmish-order-front and try to cut off anyone headin' south, and scoop up anyone ridin' east or west."

Abe tipped down his hat, pondered for a while, then said, "Captain, I don't know how good a bank-robber you are, but as a soldier you're not too bad. Look behind us and to the south."

They were small but they were down there. In fact they were smaller now than when Abe had first seen them approaching

147

from the ranch-house porch somewhat earlier, and they were doing exactly as the bank-robbing former Confederate officer had said, they were riding in a wide-spaced skirmish order heading up-country as though intending to overtake the men who had fired Cactus Ranch headquarters. So far, all they knew was that there was a fire at the ranch; they had no way of knowing it was simply their shoeing-shed. For all they knew, judging from the amount of that billowing, greasy black smoke, it could be the main-house burning.

That, it seemed to Abe, might be the circumstance which would prevent Colonel Canfield from prosecuting a fierce and deadly pursuit. He would be much more interested in trying to reach his ranch in an attempt to save as much of it as he could, than in chasing the arsonists. For all Abe knew, Canfield might not even be certain there had been arsonists, but if his strung-out riders caught Bannion and the bank-robbing former Confederate officer, riding away from the direction of the ranch, it would in all probability be a very unpleasant encounter for Abe and Grover Reasoner.

But the distance separating the two parties was much too vast. In fact as Abe held his horse to a walk and watched the tiny silhouettes down-country, it did not seem to him that he and Reasoner would have to use up their horses at all, and he was correct.

They had a smoke, appreciated Canfield's resourcefulness in the face of several uncertainties, and finally pushed on past where the skirmish-line was going to reach and saw two of those rangeriders halt down there and sit with hats tipped, peering very intently up where Abe and Grover Reasoner were riding.

"One thing to see a man," said the former officer, "and another thing to overtake him, eh, private?"

Abe chuckled. "Dead right, captain." Then, after a moment of returning the regard of those distant riders, he also said, "And don't make the mistake of thinking those bastards are going to stay home when they get that shed-fire put out."

Eventually, the pair of Cactus riders turned over westerly and closed up the skirmish line, no doubt in order to get where their employer was so they could report that they had, in fact, actually sighted a pair of men riding away from the direction of the ranch.

Abe was right; whatever else Colonel Canfield did once he reached his yard, he would return implacably to seek the men who had burned his shoeing-shed and who had promised to do much worse the next time.

The sun was darkening redly, the shadows in canyons along the farthest mountains were turning steadily more sooty, and day's end was not far distant as the pair of arsonists finally reined southward and made a steady beeline for the Weatherby place.

They had covered roughly half again as much territory on their return trip as they had used up reaching Cactus ranch. They had the Weatherby buildings in sight, though, long before those descending mountain-side shadows had spilled out across the grasslands, and when they came down behind the big log barn and swung off to corral and feed their horses, dusk was approaching, but it was not going to reach the ranchyard for another hour or hour and a half.

It was possible to stand in the centre of the yard and look off north-westerly and see a huge black mushrooming oily cloud spreading for several miles along the underbelly of the gloomy late-day sky.

12
THE UNIQUE BAND

Cal and Chet strolled into the yard carrying Winchesters but otherwise not appearing very upset nor anxious. The Weatherbys also came forth, but they remained back upon the porch.

Cal gestured. "Nice lot of black smoke," he dryly commented.

"Shoeing-shed," reported Abe. "What happened over here?"

"Not a hell of a lot. The old bastard rode in like Napoleon and I'll hand it to him, he makes an impression. Anyway, he walked his horse up out front like he was darin' us to wing him, and he said he wanted the person who had shot his rangeboss. Miz Weatherby opened the door and stood there like a banty hen, giving him glare for glare. Under different circumstances it would have been funny. She told him unless he wanted a dose of the same medicine he'd better take his border-jumpers and clear out. Then they sat and stood, and just glared at each other, until she hoisted her rifle and hauled back the hammer, then the colonel turned, spat, and started riding for the barn. We could see other fellers down there peekin' out here and there. He halted, swung down and said, 'Lady, you got five minutes to send him out, then I'll start with this here barn and burn everything right up to your porch'."

Cal looked at Chet. They both grinned and Cal said, "By gawd she fired the rifle and kicked up a big handful of gravel right in front of the old bastard. He got inside that barn faster'n I ever before saw such a big old man move." Cal paused, then said, "That's all. They was still out there when we saw the smoke, so I called down to them to say while they were over here, their ranch was bein' gutted. My gawd I never saw a bunch of men leave out of a barn so fast. They went like they was able to fly."

From the porch Sylvia Weatherby called the four of them to the house. "Supper will be on directly," she said.

They hung back a moment when Grover Reasoner said, "Listen; I doubt that the old devil will return in the night, but suppose he does?"

Cal waited. When none of the others moved, he finally said, "All right, I'll grab me something to eat then I'll take the first watch down around the barn somewhere." He scowled. "For two hours, is all, and you boys remember that!"

Then, they trooped to the main-house, and as they filed inside the first night-shadows surreptitiously and unnoticed slipped down across the yard.

Sandy came over to Abe wearing an expression of plain inquisitiveness, so Abe said, "Nothing to it. Just rode in, fired their shoeing-shed and rode out. By the way, that man you winged was their rangeboss."

Sandy stared. "It was? I thought he was just one of the riders."

Abe thought it might have been better if the lad had indeed wounded a common rangerider; his most enduring recollection of that swarthy man in the wall-bunk made him convinced that as soon as he could, the Cactus Ranch rangeboss would saddle up, arm himself, and come down here to settle with the person who had injured him. It did not seem to Abe Bannion that the fact that Sandy Weatherby was a youngster was going to make much difference. Men like that rangeboss had been just as hard and resourceful and relentless as youths as they were later in life, and they considered all youngsters tall enough to shoulder and shoot a gun, fair prey.

They had themselves been fair prey at Sandy's age. Men had been coming of age very early on the frontier ever since there had been a frontier. And although that would inevitably change in time, before it finally did change, there were going to be an awful lot more fresh granite headstones planted over youngsters between the ocean and the Missouri.

The Widow Weatherby looked up as Abe and Grover Reasoner entered her fragrant kitchen. She gestured for them to be seated near the head of the table, then turned back to the stove for a mounded platter of fried steaks and spuds. Sandy helped his mother to the extent of filling coffee cups. He was wearing his father's shellbelt and holstered big Colt. He was a little lean and young and scrawny for all that armament, but even so it looked more nearly appropriate around his middle than it had ever looked around his mother's middle.

Cal did not linger; he ate fast, drank coffee, took some meat in a piece of paper and went out the rear of the house in the direction of the barn. The others went on with their meal and hardly more than glanced up when Cal re-entered through the kitchen, his face solemn.

"Abe," he said, "you want to guess who's out there in front of the barn off-saddling and humming a hymn?"

No one spoke. They stared from Cal to Abe, and as Abe put down his eating utensils he said, "I don't believe it. He rode north. I saw his darned tracks. He was heading into the mountains."

"Well, he ain't in the mountains now, he's down in front of the barn."

Abe arose, shoved away from the table, nodded crisply and walked out of the house beside his partner.

The man down in the gloaming had his saddle athwart the tie-rack, his bridle suspended from the horn and his sweaty saddleblanket flung hair-side-up across the other gear and was leading his horse into the barn to be cuffed, stalled and fed, when Abe sang out to him.

"Hey, Mort!"

The shadowy individual halted, turned, then answered Abe in a pleasant tone. "By grabs, Mister Bannion and Mister Madison. You boys are a sight for sore eyes."

They walked on up. Sampson Mortimer smiled and offered a warm handshake as though the three of them were old friends. "I got to worrying," he told them. "I got to wonderin' if everything would work out all right for the lad and his maw. You know how a place like this can be, fellers. Lots of murderers and worse sneakin' around." He looked past at the lighted house and wrinkled his nose. "Lord, but that's a powerful good smell of cookin', gents. Just let me put up m'horse."

Abe stopped the newcomer with an out-flung arm. "The lad's fine and so is his maw. Mort, fill up in the kitchen if you got to, then get back on your horse and ride out."

The newcomer turned slowly. "Why? You boys up to meanness, are you?"

"There is a damned cow outfit four miles north-west of here that's comin' back here in the night or in the morning," explained Abe Bannion, "and there'll be fur fly. Mort, it's not your battle so I'm giving you warning. Get away before those rangemen return."

Sampson Mortimer drew himself up. "Gents, you see in front of you a tool of the Lord! I'm His buckler and His scimitar! Them as attacks the weak and innocent, the humble and the meek are fixin' to be blinded by His wrath — as dished out by me!"

Abe stood in silence watching. So did his partner, and when Sampson Mortimer had made his thunderous pronouncement, had glared them down from a fanatic's unreasoning stare, he turned and led his horse into the barn.

Cal said, "Well . . . whatever a scimitar is, now we got one, and that ought to round it out for the Weatherbys. A bank-robbing pair and another pair who — well — us, anyway, and now this burr-head called Mort." Cal grimaced. "If I was the colonel and knew what I'd be up against over here — a whole ranchful of misfits and crazies — I don't think I'd come back at all." He looked at his partner. "What'll we do with Mortimer?"

There was not much they could do; this was neither their ranch nor in particular their fight. Abe shrugged. "I think he can use a gun, and maybe we'd ought to just be thankful for that much."

Abe blew out a big breath. "Take the damned *pukutsi* back inside and introduce him around. I'll take your first watch out here . . . Right now I'd like an hour or two for figuring on things."

Mortimer came forth, finally, into the star-softened early night smelling strongly of horsesweat, which was not an especially offensive odour to rangemen who were never entirely free of it. He smiled.

"I got it figured that you boys are defendin' the meek and the innocent. There'll be a reward for you, come the blowin' of the final trumpet!"

Abe looked mildly pained. "That's nice, as long as I don't have to go right soon and collect the reward." He jerked his head. "Cal'll take you to the house."

Sampson Mortimer smiled at Abe. "About this cow outfit . . . Wouldn't be old Canfield would it?"

The partners stared. Their recollections of this strange individual was that he had been simply passing through, exactly as they had been; he had not said he knew anyone hereabouts.

Abe put it bluntly. "What about old Canfield?"

"Haven't seen him in twenty years, not since the war," replied Mortimer. "I heard from a feller we both knew back in those days that he'd come out here and settled in with a big bunch of cattle . . . You said a cow outfit from hereabouts was fixin' to make fur fly. That would be how Canfield works . . . I served under him, gents. Second Massachusetts Infantry."

Abe said, "Take him to the kitchen, Cal," and turned as they started back in the direction of the house, to watch them cross through the gloom.

That was exactly what they needed on top of all their other difficulties, a crazy man!

Abe walked to the edge of the yard and sniffed and listened and looked. As far as he could determine there was nothing out there. He hadn't expected there to be; Canfield's riders wouldn't have had time yet, to get home, put out the fire, eat supper, listen to what the rangeboss and *cosinero* had to report, catch fresh livestock and make the ride back to the Weatherby place.

He speculated on whether Canfield had left an observer around somewhere, and thought it was probable. But that was one of those open-ended thoughts a man could argue to himself with, pro and con, until the cows came home and never come up with an actual answer.

If there was a man out there he'd had an excellent chance to overhear the *pukutsi* when he'd arrived in the yard, and the observer had also had a fair opportunity to see the men Mortimer had spoken to — and to shoot them.

Nothing had happened.

Abe rolled a smoke and lit it inside his hat, strolled out behind the barn and continued on his stroll until he was over along the rear of the empty bunkhouse. If there was anyone out here, he was lying awfully close, or else he was a long way out in the night.

Each time he dragged off the cigarette he'd do it behind the hat.

The sky was high, curved, and endlessly broad and deep, and as old as it was, never-changing and timeless, it still yielded few secrets to an observer such as the burly man in the Weatherby ranch-yard who paused now and again to look up at it.

He had slept beneath it from Montana to Chihuahua and back, could find his way almost anywhere upon the horizon-less plains and through the lethal mountain chains by using the constant stars he knew the names of, but for all his years of living beneath it he knew almost nothing about it. He smoked, kept his vigil, walked sound-lessly across the yard and around behind the buildings, killed the cigarette and gave up as he had given up a thousand other times, deciding that when Fate was ready for him to know more She would see to it, and meanwhile here he was, with a half-grown boy, a widow woman, a crazy man, two renegade fugitives . . .

He laughed to himself. If it was true that all things were written in advance of a person's arrival on this earth, someone sure had one hell of a sense of humour!

A horse blew its nose across in the direction of the corrals on the north side of the barn. He stepped instantly to shadows alongside a shed upon the opposite side of the yard and waited.

There were no horses in the corrals, they were all stalled in the barn!

The horse did not make another noise; the yard, the area beyond it, and the distant night were all very quiet.

He had the tie-down yanked loose on his Colt when he decided to go around and investigate, but he had barely begun to move when he heard a walking horse over yonder and this time the sound was being repeated often enough for him to pinpoint the exact area out by the corrals where that animal was.

He stood stock-still. The oncoming horse was walking with quiet deliberation and that did not make a whole lot of sense; if Canfield were back, or if he'd had a spy over here and now the spy was moving, it seemed very unlikely that in either case the cattlemen would be this careless.

A grey shape came ambling from around the north side of the barn out into the yard, and turned abruptly heading for the doorless front opening of the log barn.

It was a loose saddlehorse!

Abe felt enormously relieved while at the

same time he also felt enormously exasperated. Someone's darned turned-out horse! It was probably an old animal, wise in the ways of people and where they stored hay and grain. Younger horses with shorter teeth shunned man as much as possible once they were turned out, but an old horse, perhaps with half his grinders left, became shrewd and wise and knowing.

The grey horse disappeared into the barn, Abe watched, then decided he had to go over there and run the old devil off or he'd start a fight with every horse he could find in the stalls, at the very best, and at the very worst the old cuss would pull down saddles, up-end barrels in his search for grain, and generally make a nuisance of himself.

From a great distance a wolf called eerily in the depthless night, his echoing call carrying far and wide. There should have been an answer and Abe instinctively listened for it as he started around the yard in the direction of the barn.

It came, from miles south-easterly, and Abe almost nodded his approval. It was too late for the mating season but at least the dog and the bitch could find one another, and spend the summer hunting together, and when the season finally came again . . .

That grey horse was a lot more "savvy"

than Abe gave him credit for being. He detected the whisperingly abrasive sounds of boot-leather over gritty dust as Abe advanced on him, and quietly went on out the back of the barn. There had been no immediate scent of grain in the barn anyway, and the overhead loft which gave off a tantalising perfume of properly-cured timothy, mountain hay, was above his head; he did not even need instinct to tell him that was an impossible area for horses.

They met around back. Abe stopped, hand on his Colt-handle. The grey horse eyed the man warily but without any actual fear since they were about sixty feet apart, then the horse strolled on out westerly through the star-bright darkness, and Abe was vindicated; the horse was old. He was nearly white now, which was the colour of dapple-greys when they got enough age on them.

13
INTO THE NIGHT!

Cal came along a half-hour after the interlude of the grey horse, stood a while in quiet conversation with his partner, chuckled over the story of the horse, nodded over his partner's recitation of the wolf-calls, and raised his head to sense the night as he said, "That damned *pukutsi* is acting as sane as you or I, in there. He's got them all believing he's an authority on just about everything." Cal shook his head; clearly, Sampson Mortimer was not only something entirely new to him in human beings, but he was also something Cal could not precisely define nor understand.

Abe let the topic lie. He was convinced that if Mort were not excessively aggravated he would be harmless, but even if this were an incorrect judgement, Abe was confident he and Cal could yank the *pukutsi*'s fangs if it came down to that. Abe was more interested in other things.

"How are Chet and his partner? Incidentally, 'Jack Jones's' real name is Grover Reasoner."

"He told you that?"

"Yeah."

Cal reverted to their earlier topic because as far as he was personally concerned, people could pick names out of the blue.

"They are acting normal enough," he said, answering Abe's earlier question. "Seems to me if we had to get into this fix, we could have done worse in pickin' fellers to be in it with . . . Leavin' Mortimer out of it, though."

Abe said, "I was wondering; when fellers got full stomachs and hours to think, sometimes they decide it's better to pull out and leave the country."

"Naw," said Cal. "Not those two." He raised his head as though listening, then dropped it again. "If that old goat Canfield comes back tonight I'll be surprised. His kind don't fight at night."

Abe cocked an eye. "You're plumb sure?"

Cal grinned; he also reddened in the darkness under the impetus of his partner's very dry comment. "Go on inside and have some coffee, I'll take the watch until midnight."

Abe nodded, willing to concede, but he made no immediate move to depart. "I keep thinking that maybe what we'd ought to do is carry the fight to Canfield like we did today. I keep wonderin' what'll happen tomorrow if the old buzzard rides down here and we're all bottled up inside the log house . . . He'll have 'burn' on his mind, Cal."

The lankier man pondered a slow reply and belatedly gave it. "Be pretty hard to fire this house; the widow's husband made damned sure no one could get across from the barn or any of the other buildings. You recollect how that looked to us in the dark? Well, by daylight it'd look even . . ."

"How about a wagon load of burning hay," said Abe, "or someone soaking the head of a fire-arrow in coal oil and flinging it onto the roof?"

Cal turned, spat, turned back and said, "What you got in mind — the two of us riding over to Canfield's place in the night?"

Abe hadn't really concentrated on this notion although it had occurred to him. But not until Cal had come out to stand with him did the idea begin to firm up. He thought its basis was sound enough; he had never been on the planning level as a soldier so he was not now entirely aware that what he was pondering came under that heading. All he knew was what instinct told him, and that, simply enough, was that when they had struck the colonel earlier in the day, they had succeeded in distracting him, and if that had worked once with the old devil, it could work again.

The main idea was to knock Canfield over onto the defensive.

Cal stood in deep thought, then finally said, "Did you figure to take Chet and what's-his-name along too."

"Reasoner. Grover Reasoner. Well; if they went with us, four would be able to make more of a ruckus over there than two, wouldn't they?"

Cal looked around. "And leave the *pukutsi* with the widow and her boy?"

Abe did not reply. He had not considered this, and now when he considered the alternatives — leaving one of the bank-robbers and taking the *pukutsi* along with them, that did not sit too well with him either.

"I don't much like the idea of leavin' those folks alone," he told Cal, "but I like it even less, leavin' them with the others while we're gone."

Cal was not that worried. "Take the bank-robbers and the *pukutsi* along. What the hell, Abe, the Weatherbys was alone before we arrived. Anyway, if we got Canfield busy over at his outfit, how's he going to make trouble down here?"

Cal was right; if they got Canfield on the defensive over at his Cactus Ranch, his last consideration would be the widow and her son back at the Weatherby place. Abe smiled slightly. "For an unbaptised feller sometimes you come up with pretty fair notions."

Cal snorted. "First damned thing I'm going to do when we get over those northerly mountains and hit a decent-sized town is hunt up a preacher and get that blasted job taken care of."

He grinned in the darkness and Abe softly laughed. Then he turned in the direction of the house and Cal continued to grin as he watched his partner depart.

A dog-coyote wailed not too far northward through the night which brought Cal's interest back to his immediate area and his exposed position. He went over into the gloom of the barn and remained over there, and when there was no answer to the dog-coyote's call, the nervous little animal ran a half mile eastward in record time and sat on his haunches to sing out again. There was no answer this time either, so the dog-coyote had to go farther before he was heard by a band and invited to join. A coyote hunting by himself was strictly limited to rodents and small game, but in a band, hunting as part of a team, he could expect to dine very well off animals as large as deer and elk, and even horses sometimes, and cattle, although a band had to be on the verge of starvation to make that kind of a kill; coyotes were sly and wise, they knew that the first time they killed domestic animals mounted men with guns would be after them in a relentless chase. How they knew such a thing was anyone's guess, but they knew it nonetheless, and they would pass up the most tempting and vulnerable kills among calves and foals.

Cal kept waiting for a band to sing out but it never happened. Evidently that lone dog-coyote was in the wrong area at the wrong time. It happened. Cal grinned. It even happened with men; by all rights he and his partner should be about a third of the way through those yonder ghostly-lighted northward mountains tonight, maybe in a decent camp with a glowing bed of coals to keep them warm in their bedrolls as they soundly slept. Instead . . .

He considered a smoke but decided against it; he was not all that much of a smoker anyway. He wandered into the barn, walked on through listening and cataloguing sounds as he moved along, emerged from the barn's rear doorway and did as Abe had done, stood a while studying the high vault of heaven.

The dog-coyote made his final sounding from so far to the east Cal could barely hear it. They were forever on the move and perhaps that was what would guarantee an eventual link-up.

Otherwise, the night was still and empty and deeply hushed as though it were much later than it actually was, and all the creatures which were unable to navigate in darkness were soundly sleeping.

Cal turned at a slight sound outside the front of the barn, stepped to one side of the barn's interior where the gloom was layers deep and began a stealthy advance up through.

A soft voice said, "Cal . . . ?"

The four of them were out there; Reasoner and his partner Chet, Sampson Mortimer and Abe Bannion. They were bundled against the creeping chill, and they were armed. Clearly, Abe's idea had prevailed.

When Cal walked out the motionless figures moved off; they had first wanted to be safely identified. Now, as they went after saddle animals they talked back and forth. Only one of them offered conversation which seemed never to quite meld with what the others were saying, except very rarely.

Sampson Mortimer.

Abe rigged out and led his horse out back to wait until his partner arrived, then he asked about the widow and her son. "Be fine," stated Cal. "They got enough guns and bullets in there to hold off the army, and they're going to take turns keepin' watch."

Clearly, Madison's conscience was clear.

They got astride. The last man from the barn was Chet. He rode around and came up even with Abe to say, "Where in hell did that looney come from? I figured he was long gone out of the country."

For some reason the bank-robber's tone annoyed Abe so all he said was, "Go ask him."

They judged the night as they rode, found nothing out in it to be leary about and eventually booted their animals into a lope.

The cold was distinctly noticeable now, finally. It would continue to be that way through what remained of the night. The darkness too, was enduring. There was star-shine and no moon, but for all that it was not really and truly a dark night; enough pale grassland reflected starlight upwards to

171

facilitate the onward progress of the armed band.

They had no plan, but as they loped overland riding all in a hastening little squad, they talked back and forth perfecting what would pass for a plan of action, but which was in fact a very simple system of Indian-type warfare. When they got within rifle-range of Cactus Ranch they intended to split up with Abe and Cal trying to get around behind the horse-barn where they could free all the corralled and stalled livestock, while the pair of bank-robbers crept to the edge of the yard and stood waiting for the first sign of someone coming out in late-night alarm, then they were to begin shooting up the place.

Sampson Mortimer was the unknown factor, so while each of them offered advice about their general scheme and the part individuals were to play in it, none of the foursome came right out with a suggestion for Mortimer.

They were less than a mile out and had hauled down to a fast walk when Sampson Mortimer said, "All right, gents; I'll capture the colonel. I'll take him in his bed-clothes if I can, but at least I'll capture him."

The others were slow and reluctant with their comments. They may have generally felt whatever Mortimer did would be fine as long as they knew what he was going to do. Whatever their private opinions, they kept them private and simply nodded or mechanically smiled at the bizarre individual riding among them.

There was a scent of pungent smoke in the night air, but there was no sign of a fire, even of coals glowing low along the ground, up where the ranch headquarters was, so evidently the shoeing-shed fire had been squelched down to nothing but ash which still smouldered giving off the acidy aroma they could easily detect a mile out.

Closer, they saw a light in the main-house, somewhere among the rooms in the back of the house. All the other buildings though were dark.

They took their horses over into that same windbreak Cal and Abe had encountered earlier, left them there, made certain of the condition and easy availability of their weapons and struck out into the yonder gloom.

Sampson Mortimer surprised them all; he was as soundless, as wraithlike and elusive as a genuine ghost. He led off the full distance to the area between the barn and the bunkhouse, and raised a rigid arm to halt them behind him when they had the yard in plain sight, and between it and them a number of Cactus Ranch buildings.

He was smiling from ear to ear when he faced about. Abe shook his head; the damned crazy-man actually thought this was fun!

"You boys do what you got to do, and I'll bring along the colonel directly," Mortimer whispered, and turned away without another word. Within moments he was lost to sight. They could not even hear him.

Grover Reasoner stepped close to where Abe and Cal were standing while they slowly studied the buildings up ahead. Reasoner said, "Two of us can neutralise that bunkhouse . . . If all those riders are inside, we can win this skirmish without a shot being fired . . . You boys going after the livestock, still?"

Abe met the ex-officer's gaze and without a word grunted at Cal and turned towards the barn. For some reason tonight, people irritated him more than they normally did. Or maybe it was just Mortimer and his manner of making Abe feel uncomfortable, and Reasoner's easy fluency about every subject that arose.

Cal trooped in his partner's wake but when they were behind the barn Cal raised a long arm to point northward where they could hear horses moving in the yonder corrals.

Abe nodded, waited until his partner had moved off in the direction of the corrals to open the gates and chouse out the animals, then he entered the barn.

The building was as black as pitch between its front and rear openings. Horses moved in their stalls and the scent was unmistakably horsy.

Abe felt no warning from his sixth-sense. His only thought so far about the possibility of Canfield having a sentry somewhere in the yard, was that there was none, and that seemed to prove that maybe Canfield wasn't such a rousing success as a soldier-officer after all.

Then a gun exploded from across the barn, the blinding light rendered Abe temporarily helpless, and the crashing roar also deafened him. He heard wood splinter very close and instinctively dropped and rolled as he frantically grabbed for his holstered Colt.

From somewhere out beyond the barn someone yelled in a high falsetto, and another gunshot sounded, but this time there was a furious fusillade of answering gunfire, and afterwards a door slammed as though someone, on their way out of the bunkhouse, after shouting to rouse up his friends, had been savagely fired upon before he could get clear of the bunkhouse door and had reeled back inside, slamming the door after himself.

Abe smelled gunpowder, heard his heart pounding, and although his vision partially cleared it was still too dark in the barn to make out anything, so he felt with his free left hand, gropingly encountered the close-spaced tines of a big manure-fork, got both legs under his body, got a firm grip on the fork balancing it like a spear, and with a grunt heaved it directly into the opposite darkness.

It struck wood and metal and someone squawked and fired towards where the fork had hit. Abe had his gun cocked and ready; he snapped off a round at the muzzle-blast yonder, then hurled himself forward as hard as he could, rolled and fired again. That time there was no answering gunshot. In fact, as he tensely waited, every gunshot-echo slowly faded out to be replaced with the same kind of deep night silence which had been in the yard when the invaders had first ridden up.

14
A DEADLY NIGHT

For Abe Bannion the fight had evolved into a simple matter of hoping he had killed someone, and in recovering full use of his sight and hearing.

Otherwise, it seemed clear that Chet and Grover Reasoner had succeeded in catching the rangeriders inside their bunkhouse as they had planned to do, which left Sampson Mortimer, and Abe hardly spared him a thought. If he got inside the main-house and didn't get himself killed in the attempt . . . Abe put the man out of his mind and felt along the Stygian darkness to ascertain whether or not he could move without noise.

He could. There was nothing around him but the frightened and nervous movement of stalled livestock, and that was more than enough to cover any sounds he might make as he crawled steadily towards the front of the barn.

There was a man across the way; what condition he was in Abe had no idea except to hope fervently the man was no longer breathing.

When he could make out the yonder yard, which was a few shades lighter than the interior of the barn, Abe stopped, listened, looked all around through blackness, and decided his part of the scheme was now to make certain the colonel's barn-sentry was out of it one way or another.

It would have been a lot easier to snake-crawl around to the right of the front opening and leave the barn to its other occupant. On the other hand if just one Cactus Ranch cowboy was loose in the night, it was a definite peril to them all.

He swore under his breath and turned back to seek a way across through the interior darkness where he would not have to betray himself with noise.

Fortunately, Canfield, like most former military officers, was a stickler for cleanliness and order; his barn was raked clean of chaff and straw every day. Abe made this discovery as he groped ahead with his left hand, constantly feeling for obstructions and finding not even any loose hay on the earthen floor to make a whisper-rattle as he snake-crawled on his way.

He was perspiring inside his shirt and jacket and it was far from warm even in the barn, this night. He was also getting progressively more nervous as he came towards the north side of the barn where that gunman had been, and probably still was.

He had reason to be anxious; that sentry had fired at him without one hint of warning and for all the sentry knew he might have been one of the colonel's men from the bunkhouse. He had no illusions at all about what would happen if he and the border-jumper met this close in a second confrontation, so he kept his right hand with the cocked Colt in it, slightly ahead of his body and sheltered by his left hand and arm as he belly-crawled.

It was as though he and his adversary were the only ones still willing to make a fight of it; beyond the barn the night was hushed and deathly still. If there was other human activity out there, no one seemed certain of it, and Abe Bannion least of all was immediately concerned.

What had actually happened had been about as he had surmised earlier. In response to that gunshot inside the barn a cowboy had tried to rush forth from the bunkhouse with a gun in hand, and had been driven back in confused astonishment when Chet and Grover Reasoner had fulfilled their part of the scheme by blazing away towards the front of the bunkhouse. Now, the men inside were effectively bottled up. They were like caged cougars and this was easy to imagine since their hardened employer would hire only men who would fight at the drop of a hat. On the other hand they were not fools, otherwise they would have tried again to leave the log bunkhouse.

Elsewhere, there was no way of knowing what might be transpiring. None of the other outlaw-nightriders had ever been confident of their ability to predict what Sampson Mortimer might do, and for the present they were too busy with their work to care about speculating. That light which had been burning over at the main-house when they had ridden in, was still burning, and the silence over there was just as enduring now as it had also been earlier. There was no inkling at all of what may have transpired over there.

Cal was northward in the night, somewhere. He had opened corral gates and had in fact been chousing out loose-stock when that sentry inside the barn had fired at Abe. After that Cal left it up to the loose-stock to find their own way out of the corrals and stealthily made his way back to the north log wall of the barn to lean close in an effort to hear, but there was no sound in the barn after Abe's gunshot and the loud squawk of his invisible adversary, so Cal cautiously made his way up in the direction of the barn's front, and there he stood, gun in hand, able to see all the way up through the yard past the outbuildings to the mainhouse, without discerning any movement at all.

He thought he knew about where Reasoner and Chet were, but looking across in that direction showed him nothing. He knew for a fact no one had exited from the bunkhouse which meant Chet and Reasoner had succeeded. As for Abe, there was cause for worry and Cal gently eased along the front of the barn.

Those gunshots had seemed to come from down through and nearer the rear exit of the barn. He reasoned that no one would try to escape in that direction, they would come up towards the front opening where there had not seemed to be any obstacles.

Maybe his reasoning was good. It was never tested. After a long wait in the heavy and ominous silence of the yard, he heard a whisper of movement inside the barn and sank to one knee, raised his Colt and with his left hand holding to the log jamb of the doorway, he patiently awaited the next sound in order to be able to place the man in there.

There was no more sound of any kind. Time dragged and tension in the ranch-yard drew out perilously thin and menacing. Finally, a rangerider with frayed patience called from the bunkhouse.

"Who's out there? Is that you fellers from the Weatherby place?"

From a short distance an echoing answer was returned, thick with rough irony. "What's the matter, fellers, you didn't expect the widow to have friends?"

That ended the exchange. Whatever the purpose of that bottled-up man in the bunkhouse may have been in originally yelling forth, he did not pursue the verbal exchange and neither did anyone else.

Abe, who had heard both shouts, was two-thirds of his way across the barn and halted briefly until the exchange had been completed, then raised his head like a cautious lizard and sensed his black surroundings. Once, he thought he heard something along the front wall, and flattened. The sound did not come again for quite a while, then it sounded as though someone were dragging himself toward the opening and Abe turned slightly, twisted his prone body and swung his sixgun making a hard effort to be certain where the noise-maker was.

The sound seemed to stop and remain that way through an interval, then start up again. It was very soft, almost too soft to be detected.

Abe debated. He thought the man who was crawling up there by the doorway was either injured and had to rest after each dragging movement, or else was close enough to escaping out the front of the barn to be able to afford pauses which might prevent his adversary inside the building from locating him. Either way he swung the Colt and waited. When the faint sound returned he tracked it and when it stopped he held the gun steady, waiting for one last hint before squeezing off a shot.

The man probably deserved a warning; that was the chivalrous thing to do. It was also the most foolhardy thing to do. Abe waited, shallowly breathing, body clammy, trigger-finger lightly tensed. When the movement came very briefly up near the jamb, he squeezed off his gunshot.

The noise was triply thunderous because of all the other silence in the night. A man bawled in angry surprise from the front barn opening and fired back, but his shot was high and wide. It hit wood near the rear opening on the south side.

Those two gunblasts panicked the stalled horses. They kicked and pawed and hit walls and doors in terror, and all this noise temporarily diverted Abe. When some of that noise subsided, though, he checked his estimates and came to the conclusion that the man who had fired at him had been already around the corner of the barn, on the outside.

He cocked the Colt and waited, not daring to move for fear he would make enough noise to draw more gunfire. A harsh voice suddenly spoke fervently but quietly.

"Hey, you son of a bitch, you come out of there with your hands empty or I'm comin' in there and stomp some wadding out of you!"

Abe remained rigid for a moment, then slowly let the gunbarrel tip down, slowly allowed his rigid body to loosen, and gradually sucked back a big breath of cold night air.

"Cal," he said, almost plaintively. "You danged idiot!"

For a moment there was silence from out front, then Cal said, "Well, hell; darned good thing you can't hit the side of a barn even from the inside of it! . . . Who else is in there?"

Abe turned his head. If that sentry had been able, no doubt by now he would have blazed away at Abe. "Darned if I know who he is, and I'm not even sure he's still breathin'. Come on in," he invited his partner, "and we'll look him up."

"Yeah, sure," muttered Cal from the safety of the outside log wall. "If you want to crawl down some feller's gunbarrel go right ahead, I ain't going to."

Abe twisted more. He called softly across the barn. There was no reply and he had rather thought there wouldn't be, so he resumed crawling, and this time he was not careful of the noise he made.

Every time his eyes had become more accustomed to the blackness, gunfire had temporarily blinded him, and now as he felt something yielding up ahead and raised his gunhand as well as his head, he could not see what he had touched nor what he was ready to shoot at.

Behind him and up at the doorway Cal called. "What are you doing in there?"

Abe felt the limpness and the warmth, eased up and leaned over and saw the pale round face looking steadily up at him. The man was dead.

"Hey; what the hell are you doing in there, Abe?" Cal sounded worried. "Speak up or

I'll come in and . . ."

"There's a dead guy over here," Abe said quietly, and sat up to dust the front of his jacket and shirt. He eased off the dog of his Colt and leathered the weapon, then leaned for an even closer look. The man in front of him was flat out on his back, eyes wide, features perfectly composed, and midway down there was a ragged hole in his chest, plumb centre.

Two feet away against the wall was that manure-fork Abe had hurled like a spear. He remembered the sentry yelling out when the fork had struck near him.

"Abe . . . ?"

He turned doorward. "Come on in, Cal, and keep to the north wall, and doggone you don't shoot that gun again!"

Abe got stiffly to his feet, shook himself, pushed his shirt-tail in, re-arranged his jacket and watched his partner materialise in the darkness, look past at the dead man, then lean for a closer examination.

"Oh, hell," Cal breathed, and straightened back. "What was he doin' in here?"

"Sentry, I expect," said Abe. "But he didn't act too smart; he should have snuck out of here when he heard me comin' in."

"Maybe the colonel don't hire 'em for bein' smart, just for being quick-triggered."

They left the dead man and returned to the front of the barn where the yard showed several degrees brighter because of that glass-clear overhead starshine.

There was nothing out there; no sound, no movement, no silhouettes which could have belonged to other men. It made Abe feel alone except for Cal. He said, "Somebody's got to get the talkin' started."

Cal said nothing, he simply stood there sniffing at the night like an old hunting dog, and kept his drawn Colt hanging loosely at his side.

Abe cupped his hands facing in the direction of the bunkhouse. "Hey, you Canfield riders: You want to come out unarmed with your hands out front, or do you want to stay in there and get roasted when we fire the bunkhouse?"

For a long time there was no response. In fact the silence dragged on for so long it began to seem that there was not going to be a response, then a muffled deep, rough voice called back. "All right, we'll come out unarmed. No guns, now, damn you fellers. We're comin' out without no weapons like you said."

"Straight out front of the bunkhouse," sang out Abe. "Not left nor right, and don't any of you try fading out. Walk dead ahead and stop in the centre of the yard. No guns and no boot-knives — no nothin' you understand? Now come out!"

The silence drew out again and the bunkhouse door remained closed. It was not hard to imagine the reluctance of some of those rangeriders to surrender like this, and walk out against men they had never seen, without weapons of any kind. They probably argued, but the threat hanging over their heads was the kind that permitted no room for compromise; either they came out unarmed and at the mercy of their enemies, or they got roasted inside their log bunkhouse.

Finally, the door opened and although no one stepped out immediately, a man shoved out his hand and arm, and gingerly followed that up by exposing half himself, and finally walking forth into full sight, both arms pushed out in front.

15
NORTH NOT SOUTH!

There were only three of them and that made Abe suspicious enough as he strolled over to look more closely at them. Cal, too, acted wary as a wild horse and when Grover Reasoner counted them and swore as he stepped into plain view upon the opposite side of the yard, and noisily cocked his gun, Abe said, "Where's the rest of the crew?"

The unshaven red-headed and red-faced man standing wide-legged and looking defiant who faced Abe, answered curtly. "This is all we got, except for a feller out there by the barn somewhere and the rangeboss in bed wounded inside. And there was another feller, but he quit this morning, drew his pay and rode off."

The red-headed man gazed steadily at Abe. "You was in the barn?" he asked. "Was that you shootin' in the barn . . . ?"

Cal broke in roughly to say, "He's dead, if you're worried about the sentry inside the barn. Shot through the brisket and dead as a lousy stone."

The red-headed man did not act particularly upset. He looked at his sombre companions and said, "Don't leave too many, does it?"

No one answered and Chet walked over looking pugnacious to begin a rough and thorough search. The men were like ghosts in that eerie yard limned only by starshine, rumpled and dirty and troubled-looking.

Abe waited until Chet had completed his fruitless search for concealed weapons then glanced past the captives in the direction of the main-house. It was awfully quiet over there; that lamp was still burning in one of the rear rooms. Nothing seemed to have changed at all, in that direction, since the fight had started more than an hour earlier.

Abe was a little uncomfortable about going over there. So evidently was Grover Reasoner because when he saw the direction of Abe's gaze, he said, "Leave him be; whatever he's up to in time it'll come out. I don't feel much like butting in."

Abe did not much like the idea of butting in either, but neither did he especially care about lingering over here at the Canfield place a moment longer than he had to. Abe and his partner had engaged in a number of colourful enterprises over the years but neither of them had ever been much of a swashbuckler and still could not claim that distinction. On the other hand, they could hardly just ride off with their captives and leave Sampson Mortimer over here all alone. He had come with them — whether they had wanted him along or not — and he had voluntarily offered to help them, so they owed him.

Abe looked at Grover. "Have you seen Mort since he left us a while back?"

Grover hadn't. "Nope; but then I didn't keep watch neither. Chet and I had our own chores to do." Grover looked once more in the direction of the main-house. "He'll be along directly; whatever's happened in there will come out."

Abe and Cal exchanged a look and the taller man turned cautious. "A man can get shot dead by accident in a mess like this."

Abe could have agreed with that; he and his own partner had exchanged accidental shots. If it happened again over at the Canfield residence, maybe this next time someone who accidentally fired first might get lucky.

Abe turned on his heel. "Come along," he growled and without another word Cal followed on across through the gloom in the direction of the main-house.

No one called them back nor offered to accompany them. Chet and Grover had a perfectly valid excuse; one of them went looking for rope while the other one kept their disgruntled captives under guard, and no one paid the slightest attention to the paunchy man who stealthily emerged from the rear of the cook-shack, back where the *cosinero* had his room, lugging a heavy old carpetbag with leather-reinforced corners, wearing a dented derby hat and a much-too-small coat as he picked his careful way on around in the direction of the opposite range out behind the barn.

No one was going to miss the ranch cook and as far as anyone would ever know he had taken no part in the fight at Cactus Ranch. Why he felt so strongly impelled to secretly saddle a horse and race away in order to effectively disappear was never resolved either; not that it made much difference. Nor were people around the fringes of the low desert likely to try and prise into someone's past; it wasn't healthy, advisable, and it could also start someone else's interest in *their* pasts!

No one knew the cook was actually gone until the following day and by then his importance had dwindled to zero.

192

That night — or very early and very dark morning — when Abe and Cal reached the porch of the main-house the cook's presence on the ranch was not even considered as they went along the front of the house, guns in hand, hugging the front wall and making almost no noise.

They halted at the steel-reinforced oaken front door. Abe stretched his gun-hand, pushed with the tip of his Colt-barrel, and to his astonishment that fortress-like door swung inward on silent spindles.

He looked around. Cal leaned to peek inside. The house was darker in the front parlour than the interior of the log barn had been. Cal drew back and whispered.

"Old bastard's probably settin' on the sofa in there with a sawed-off shotgun, just waiting."

Abe said, "In that case, you being skinnier, you'd ought to go in first."

Cal leaned close to whisper again. "Hell, no. I never been baptised, remember, and you know what happens to folks when they die if they never been baptized! . . . You go, and I'll make darned sure he never gets to shoot anyone else as soon as I see his gun-blast."

Abe straightened around, pushed back his hat and leaned, Colt rising as he exposed part of his upper body and his face to look inside.

It was too dark to identify much; the big room was furnished with dark leather and dark wood. The hearth was cold, but there was black stain up the stone front to indicate many a fire had burned there.

Cal gave a little nudge and Abe pulled back. "Quit pushin' damn it," he hissed.

"Step in," whispered Cal. "He's not there or he'd have shot at you."

"If you're in such a big damned hurry to get in there and . . ."

"We can't stand out here all night, can we, confound it?"

Abe glared, then turned back, cocked his Colt, waited for a reaction and when none came, he did as Cal had admonished, he stepped around and into the big old dark parlour.

Nothing happened. There was not a sound throughout the house. It would have been better if there had been something, a curse, a gunshot, a shout, something hurled in the direction of the intruders. Instead the silence continued and Abe eased to one side, Cal moving over in the opposite direction. They functioned like well-trained bear-dogs; without a spoken word both knew exactly what to do, and moved easily to do it.

They could see light in a yonder hallway. It was coming from somewhere in the rear of the house. Without noise they moved to the hallway entrance and crouched low to peek around. The hallway was also empty so they moved on, one behind the other, and made their way to the room where the light was glowing. Here, they could easily smell cigar-smoke. Evidently Colonel Canfield lived in the rear rooms of his ranch-house, probable had his bedroom and office back here.

It was a correct assumption. Abe turned, gestured, and as Cal whisked across the open doorway from which the light was spilling into the hallway, Abe swung ahead with his cocked Colt making a lethal sweep.

Nothing happened.

Abe let his breath out slowly. "There they are," he said, moving heavily forward into the lighted room.

Cal came from the opposite side of the hall doorway and halted as soon as he could see.

Colonel Canfield, whom neither Abe nor Cal had ever before seen in their lives, was sitting at his desk leaning back in the straight old-fashioned ladderback chair. He was staring without any expression at all across the room where Sampson Mortimer was slouching back upon a horsehair black-leather sofa. There was a triangular, offset bayonet, heavily blued and looking almost shiny new in the lampglow, pinning Mortimer to the horsehair sofa through the centre of his chest. Mortimer was staring as steadily at Colonel Canfield as the colonel was staring at him.

Cal puffed out his cheeks and emitted a long breath. "Gawddamn," he muttered. "How in hell did he do that?"

Abe said, "Threw it. See those dowels in the wall behind his desk; darned bayonet was hangin' there, and when Mort came around and stepped to the sofa, the old bastard threw it and pinned him neat as a pin."

Abe pointed to the gun on the floor near Mortimer's feet. "If he'd cocked the gun before he walked in here there'd have been a gunshot when the weapon hit the floor, more'n likely."

Abe turned his back on the dead *pukutsi* and faced the big, heavy-jawed older man slouching at the desk. He leaned, pushed aside a pearl-handled small revolving-barrelled pistol and placed both his hands atop the desk to stare.

Cal came over, then Cal stepped around the side of the big old littered desk and halted where he could see the way the colonel was sitting. Cal reached gently, and pushed. Canfield's slouch became gently more pronounced and Cal looked puzzled.

"The old bastard's dead," he announced. "Abe, there's not a mark on him that I see." As he finished making this observation Cal went closer, grabbed the big old man's coat front and eased the body back as he also pushed the chair away from the desk.

From out front Grover Reasoner called, then came clumping down the long hallway herding that red-headed rangeman ahead of him. As soon as they entered the office and saw the pair of corpses, the red-headed man said, "They told him. They told the colonel over at Albuquerque, and last autumn up at Raton when we took some cattle up . . . they told him his heart was going to up and quit one of these days unless he stopped bein' so active . . . Hell; he must've moved awful fast for a man his heft and age when he flung that lousy bayonet."

Grover punched the red-headed man from behind with a pistol-barrel. "Tell 'em," he ordered.

The red-headed man shrugged and turned from gazing at his dead employer. "No reason not to, now," he said, and gazed frankly at Abe. "We got maybe fifteen red-back cows belonged to that widow-lady and her boy. The colonel paid five dollars a head each time we brought one in. Same — five dollars — for each horse, too. Only horse we left was an old buggy-animal that was born the same darned year I was."

Abe smiled at the rangerider. "You want to take what's left of your crew and return the widow-lady's critters — and throw in maybe another thirty, forty head for fair measure, and maybe six or eight good horses, too?"

The red-headed man looked from Abe to Cal, then said, "Well, he's dead ain't he? That means we are out of work, don't it?"

Cal smiled too. "For a dumb son of a bitch you're gettin' smarter by the minute. Abe, we may not have to shoot 'em after all."

The red-headed man looked long at Cal before turning his attention back to Abe. "Yeah, I'll do that. I'll take the other boys and make up a decent bunch for the widow-lady. Horses too. With a few more head flung in for good measure . . . Providin' there won't be nothing wrong with us fellers roundin' up a few dozen head for ourselves and hazing them north out of the country with us."

Abe saw Grover looking at him, and ignored this to nod in the direction of the red-headed man. "Help yourself. If you get caught it'll be your butt."

The red-headed man said nothing but he gave Abe a wise and knowing smile. Clearly, stealing cattle was not something he had never done before. He gestured. "What about all this — the house and barn and all the colonel's private gatherings?"

"Just take the livestock down to the widow-lady," said Abe, "then pick up your wages in another bunch, and the fellers with you load that gunshot rangeboss in a wagon and take him with you and shag your tails plumb out of the countryside. Red, if you ever come back, we'll kill you."

The cowboy was brisk as he turned towards Grover. "All right if I go out and tell the other fellers the colonel's dead and we're plumb out of work?"

Reasoner holstered his gun, stepped back, and after the red-headed man had departed he faced Cal and Abe with a rueful look. "You expect that old dead bastard at the desk had kinfolk?" he asked. "I never even dreamed I'd be in this kind of a mix-up." He kept looking at Abe. "What happens to the ranch and what those bloodsuckers leave of it?"

Abe turned to leave the room. "Darned if I know. Help yourself, Grover, if that's what you got in mind."

"You boys don't want it?"

Abe paused and looked at his partner. Cal shook his head. "I don't mind ridin' for cowmen," he stated, "but I sure as hell don't want to *be* one."

They returned to the yard and interestingly enough during their absence the sky had brightened, there was a pearly soft burnished look to the eastern horizon and the cold had seemed to become more intense although there was a clear sky overhead to indicate that by mid-morning it would be warm and golden again.

Chet was leaning on the tie-rack talking with the other two captives from the bunkhouse. Chet had holstered his Colt and the three of them were smoking as they talked. Chet looked up. "Everything all right in there?"

"Sure," replied Abe, striding towards the barn as he replied. "Go on inside and see for yourself."

He and Cal went over as far as the barn but did not enter it. There was nothing they wanted to see in there, especially not now that the night of a new day made visibility better.

They went down the north side of the barn and kept right on walking until they were almost back to the windbreak where the horses had been patiently dozing for half the night.

"I tell you for a lousy fact," exclaimed Abe as he snugged up his saddle and swung across it, "I'm never going to take that darned west fork in the road again no matter what. By now we should have been a third of the way on across the mountains."

"Wasn't my idea," said Cal, and earned a bleak stare as he mounted and wheeled his horse to lead off back in the direction of the Weatherby place.

Abe followed for a short distance then pointed northward. "In case you've went blind, those are the mountains we got to cross."

Cal looked and scowled. "You're not going to go tell the widow-lady she's got some livestock comin' and that her neighbour's dead?"

"Do I look like the Good Fairy? Turn your darned horse and let's head for that ghost-town to finish gatherin' our goods, then head straight north. By evenin' today we'd ought to be about where we should have been last night."

Cal looked exasperated but he turned over

in the direction of Paso Fino. For a long while as they rode through the cold morning he was thoughtfully silent, then he finally wagged his head and spoke out.

"I never saw a feller die like that before. Did you?"

"Run through by a Union bayonet? Yeah. But I never saw anyone throw one of those darned things like it was an In'ian lance. You know, by golly, I wish Canfield had hung around a little longer, I'd have liked to talk to him."

Cal snorted. "Talked hell; that old devil would have stuck you to the wall if you'd gone in there afor the *pukutsi* went in. Hey, we should have taken the *pukutsi*'s dutch oven and fry-pan."

Abe was not interested, he could see the empty town and its weathered rooftops appearing out of the golden glow of new day sunlight. Sampson Mortimer was someone he would just as soon not have to remember very often and if they'd taken some of the *pukutsi*'s gatherings every time they cooked up a meal they would be reminded.

The sun was as large as a wagon-wheel, the air was clear, warmth was building and southward down across the distant low desert where they had made the crossing, a brassy sort of coppery glow hung haze-like to indicate that although springtime was still over the border-country, summer was not too distant.

Northward though the high mountains looked cool and green and inviting. Beyond them lay an altogether different world. Abe rolled a smoke, thought of the handsome black-headed widow-woman, of her spirited beanpole of a son, and lit up, half smiling. Someday — maybe — he might come back. Maybe.

ABOUT THE AUTHOR

Lauran Paine who, under his own name and various pseudonyms has written over 900 books, was born in Duluth, Minnesota, a descendant of the Revolutionary War patriot and author, Thomas Paine. His family moved to California when he was at an early age and his apprenticeship as a Western writer came about through the years he spent in the livestock trade, rodeos, and even motion pictures where he served as an extra because of his expert horsemanship in several films starring movie cowboy Johnny Mack Brown. In the late 1930s, Paine trapped wild horses in Northern Arizona and even, for a time, worked as a professional farrier. Paine came to know the Old West through the eyes of many who had been born in the previous century and he learned that Western life had been very different from the way it was portrayed on the screen. "I knew men who had killed other men," he later recalled. "But they were the exceptions. Prior to and during the Depression, people were just too busy eking out an existence to indulge in Saturday-night brawls." He served in the U.S. Navy in the Second World War and began writing for Western pulp magazines following his discharge. It is interesting to note that all of his earliest novels (written under his own name and the pseudonym Mark Carrel) were published in the British market and he soon had as strong a following in that country as in the United States. Paine's Western fiction is characterized by strong plots, authenticity, an apparently effortless ability to construct situation and character, and a preference for building his stories upon a solid foundation of historical fact. *Adobe Empire* (1956), one of his best novels, is a fictionalized account of the last twenty years in the life of trader William Bent and, in an off-trail way, has a melancholy, bittersweet texture that is not easily forgotten. *Moon Prairie* (1950), first published in the United States in 1994, is a memorable story set during the mountain man period of the frontier. In later novels such as *The Homesteaders* (1986) or *The Open Range Men* (1990), he showed that the special magic and power of his stories and characters had only matured along with his basic themes of changing times, changing attitudes, learning from experience, respecting nature, and the yearning for a simpler, more moderate way of life. His most recent Western novels include *Tears of the Heart, Lockwood* and *The White Bird.*

We hope you have enjoyed this Large Print book. Other Thorndike, Wheeler, and Chivers Press Large Print books are available at your library or directly from the publishers.

For information about current and upcoming titles, please call or write, without obligation, to:

Publisher
Thorndike Press
295 Kennedy Memorial Drive
Waterville, ME 04901
Tel. (800) 223-1244

or visit our Web site at:

http://gale.cengage.com/thorndike

OR

Chivers Large Print
published by BBC Audiobooks Ltd
St James House, The Square
Lower Bristol Road
Bath BA2 3SB
England
Tel. +44(0) 800 136919
email: bbcaudiobooks@bbc.co.uk
www.bbcaudiobooks.co.uk

All our Large Print titles are designed for easy reading, and all our books are made to last.